Praise for *Tell Us*

'When you start reading a Dana Reinhardt book, it's like discovering a new friend. By the time you've turned the final page it's like saying goodbye to your best friend, and I can think of nothing better to ask of a writer.'

Markus Zusak, author of *The Book Thief*

'I promise you'll fall in love with River Dean, even though he's a faker, a stalker, a non-driver, a bad dancer, a bad friend and a co-dependent mess. He's funny and he's true. His heart is smashed six different ways and he's trying to mend it with tacos and lies – but isn't that true of all of us?'

E. Lockhart, *New York Times*-bestselling author of *We Were Liars*

'A heartfelt tale that elevates truth over passion and friends over lovers. Reinhardt keeps it real. Much respect.'

Matthew Quick, author of *The Silver Linings Playbook*

'A sharp-witted, hilarious, and addicting novel about being lost and discovering your best self. Highly recommended!'

Adam Silvera, *New York Times*-bestselling
author of *More Happy Than Not*

'Oh, how I love a novel where the hero ties himself up, Houdini style, and dives into his own predicament. Once again Dana Reinhardt has written a charming, compassionate, very clever comedy, and this one reminds us how a big lie can reveal the truth.'

Laura McNeal, author of *Dark Water*

'*Tell Us Something True* is hope, it is humanity, it is original, funny, wrenching, real, and intelligently surprising.'

Beth Kephart, author of *Small Damages* and *Going Over*

TELL US
SOMETHING
TRUE

DANA REINHARDT

ROCK THE BOAT

A Rock the Boat Book

First published in the United Kingdom and the Commonwealth
by Rock the Boat, an imprint of Oneworld Publications, 2016

Copyright © Dana Reinhardt 2016

The moral right of Dana Reinhardt to be identified as the Author
of this work has been asserted by her in accordance with the
Copyright, Designs and Patents Act 1988

ISBN 978-1-78074-973-0
ISBN 978-1-78607-011-1 (ebook)

Printed and bound in Great Britain by Clays Ltd, St Ives plc
Book design by Stephanie Moss

Oneworld Publications
10 Bloomsbury Street
London WC1B 3SR
England

For Daniel. Fate, luck, whatever the force
that brought us together,
I am grateful every day for you.

ONE

Up until the afternoon Penny Brockaway dumped me in the middle of Echo Park Lake, I didn't believe in fate.

Before you start conjuring visions of me in a zippered body bag sinking to the bottom of that filthy water, I mean to say she dumped me, as in she broke up with me, as in she took my heart and stomped on it while wearing a pair of those clunky boots she liked, and then she got behind the wheel of her SUV and she drove over it before picking up what flattened pieces were left and tossing them in the compost bin.

We took out one of those little pedal boats.

I did all the pedaling.

We'd heard about the boats from her best friend Vanessa, who'd told Penny you could take boats into the middle of Echo Park Lake and doesn't that sound romantic? To be out in the middle of a lake with the person you love?

It didn't sound all that great to me, but Penny wanted to do it, and doing anything with Penny was romantic.

Watching her brush her hair. Or tie her shoe. Or blow a bubble with her blue sugar-free gum. I didn't need to be in a boat in the middle of some fake lake to feel all warm and fuzzy about Penny. I was just as happy sitting on the back steps of her house watching her three-legged dog try to outrun the sprinklers. Or keeping her company while she babysat her fat little brother, Ben.

But she wanted to go on those goddamn boats. I should have just said no, but I didn't. And then it took us four months to find a Saturday afternoon we could drive out to Echo Park, and we finally did, and when we got there we had to wait forty-five minutes for a boat, and we finally got a red one, and we climbed in and I pedaled us out to the middle of the lake, and that's when she said, "Riv," followed by a big sigh and a longing look back at the dock, where I'd paid some teenager in a stupid vest twenty bucks for the privilege of renting the boat on which my girlfriend was about to dump me. "I just can't do this anymore."

The funny thing is, I thought: *But I've done all the pedaling.*

What happened next is sort of a blur. Some people talk about having an out-of-body experience in moments of tragedy, like they're somewhere up in the clouds looking down at a miniature version of themselves. Some people describe feeling like they're underwater, where everything moves in a distorted slow motion. Me? My body turned to ice and my head caught on fire. Like I was some reject superhero with totally useless, self-harming powers.

She obviously said more. She must have. But for however many minutes—or maybe it was hours, because it was like the sun shifted, the light out on the water changed— for whatever time passed between when she said *I can't do this anymore* and *It's just that you aren't really . . . the kind of person I think I deserve,* I didn't hear a thing. And I don't think whatever she said is living somewhere hidden inside me, like those little black boxes on airplanes that record all the critical data, because I've searched deep. I've practically meditated on it, and all I come back with is silence.

"What kind of person do you deserve, Pen?" I wish I'd asked this in a deep voice, with maybe an Argentinean accent, something manly, instead of croaking it like a frog. Something was happening to me that made it hard to speak.

"Someone . . . I don't know. . . ." She looked back at the dock again. Was it that guy in the vest? Was that who she felt she deserved? Someone who sold tickets for "romantic" pedal boats where love goes to die? "Someone . . . with more interest in stuff."

"Interest in stuff."

"Just more . . . I don't know . . . more . . ." Usually Penny was smart and quick and funny. So I knew she was struggling, which felt good, I guess, because it was clear she hadn't spent time rehearsing what she wanted to say, so I could hold on to the hope that she was acting on an impulse.

"More . . . ?"

"Riv, stop making this so hard on me."

I wish we'd taken a rowboat. I'd have dropped the oars. Then we could have sat out in the middle of Echo Park Lake forever, or at least until she realized she was making a terrible mistake.

But then she started to pedal. Slowly. Like she was hoping I wouldn't notice, except that when she moved her pedals, mine moved too, they were connected. Simpatico. Just like we used to be.

The dock and the idiot in the vest were drawing nearer. I'd paid for a full hour. We'd been gone fifteen minutes.

"Look," she said as her pedaling hit its stride. She bit her upper lip in that way I found totally adorable. Penny never wore lip gloss like all the other girls. Why try to improve on perfection? "You don't reflect. You don't think about things. You just follow along and do what you think you're supposed to. You don't even try to understand yourself and your issues, because, you know, River, you *do* have issues—"

"I love you, Penny."

"I know you love me. I'm pretty clear on that."

"I mean, I really, really love you."

"That's sweet, but—"

"That's sweet?"

"Let's just—"

"Is this because of Vanessa? Because I think when she told you about going out on a lake with someone you love, she meant you and her."

"You're crazy."

"I am. About you." I wish I hadn't said that. God, it was

4

so tacky. Right out of one of those crap romantic comedies Penny made me watch.

She rolled her eyes. I wasn't even looking at her, I couldn't bear to, but I knew she rolled her eyes. As she pedaled us up to the dock, the kid in the vest called out, "Toss me the rope."

I clenched it in my fists.

"Let him have the rope, River."

"No."

"He needs the rope to pull us in."

"No."

"Whatever," she said as she stepped out of the boat. She had to lunge to bridge the distance. She grabbed the arm of the kid in the vest as I sat alone in the boat with the rope in my hands.

"Come on, River."

"No."

I didn't know what I was doing or why, but I'd made up my mind somehow. I wasn't getting out of that boat.

"I want to go now."

"So go."

"We're in Echo Park. How are you going to get home?"

"I'll take the bus."

"Very funny."

"I mean it."

"You've never taken the bus in your life."

"So?"

She sighed and threw a look at the kid in the vest, like: *What am I supposed to do with this guy?*

"Fine," she said, digging in her purse for her car keys and then dangling them in front of her. "I'm leaving now. Last call for a ride home."

"Pass."

"Good-bye, River. Good luck with . . ." She gestured to the lake. ". . . everything."

TWO

I'm not proud to admit that I never bothered to get my driver's license.

Most kids who grow up in LA start dreaming of driving as soon as they're old enough to dream. But when I turned sixteen, I didn't go to the DMV like everyone else, and then I turned seventeen and it sort of became a thing: I was the guy who didn't have a license. Why? Well, I never needed one. I fell in love with Penny Brockaway when we were fifteen and then she turned sixteen a month before I did, and she got her license like everybody else, so I didn't need to know how to drive, because I had her, until the day I found myself stuck in the middle of Echo Park Lake, thirteen freeway miles away from home. It turned out to be only ten miles on surface streets, 10.2 to be precise, which I learned because I walked all 10.2 of them.

I had a phone. There were people I could have called. Mom. Or Leonard, though I knew he was at work. I could have called Will or Luke or Maggie; they'd have relished the opportunity to drive me home from a breakup with Penny. Hell, I could have called a taxi. But I didn't want to face anyone, not even some cabdriver I'd never have to see again in all my life.

I finally threw the kid the rope, and I got out of that boat, and he told me I owed him another twenty bucks because I'd cut into my second hour just sitting there thinking, and I reached into my wallet and gave it to him, because I couldn't bear failing to meet anyone else's expectations.

I set out on foot. I won't lie to you—I had no idea where I was going. I had never been to Echo Park. I rarely went east of Fairfax.

I am not, nor was I ever, a member of the Boy Scouts of America or anything, yet I somehow knew that west was toward the sun, which had begun a lazy descent. This day was going to take its time ending.

I walked through Filipinotown, Thai Town, Koreatown. Past shops selling bright plastic buckets and flowered umbrellas and silk pajamas and spices and fish and radios and futons. I didn't stop for noodles or dumplings or shave ice. I couldn't remember when or what I'd eaten last: typically I had a monster appetite, so it was saying something that I didn't buy so much as a Boba tea.

Finally, on a particularly dreary stretch of midcity Pico Boulevard, I started to lose it, thinking about my haircut. We'd gone to the Rudy's in Venice, just last week, and Penny'd told the guy who cut my hair, Jasper, I think his name was, exactly what to do. *Keep it shaggy. Take some off the back; he looks like he's got a mullet.* She had her hand on my neck when she said that, and she was running her fingers through the back of my hair, pulling on it a little to illustrate her point.

How do you go from caressing the ends of someone's hair to dumping him in Echo Park Lake in the span of a week?

What had happened was hitting me with the force of an earthquake, but not one of those minor ones LA gets where you sometimes have to pretend you felt it.

It was right at that moment, when I was about to fall apart, in the middle of the empty sidewalk, which had probably never seen a pedestrian, as the sun finally disappeared in front of me and there was nothing left to guide my way, that I saw it.

The sign.

Painted black and fading on a tattered white awning:
A SECOND CHANCE.

Like Vegas or Times Square, a big, bright, flashing neon sign, that's how I saw it—a *sign*, beckoning me: *Hey, you! River Anthony Dean! Seventeen-year-old nobody without a license or a girlfriend! Over here! This way!*

Now I understood why I'd held on to that rope, why I wouldn't step out of that boat, why I wouldn't take Penny's offer of a ride home, why I didn't stop for noodles or dumplings or shave ice. I needed to arrive on this block at this moment and see A SECOND CHANCE shining like a beacon in my darkness.

This sign was put here for me.

I stood underneath the awning and faced a pair of dirty glass doors with a piece of paper taped to one of them:

HERE: *Is where you belong.*

THIS: *Is where change begins.*

NOW: *Is the time.*

COME ON IN.

I walked through an empty reception area to another set of doors and pushed through those, continuing to feel a pull toward something important. Something with the power to right the course of my catastrophic afternoon.

I found myself in a large windowless room with a circle of metal folding chairs and about a dozen people. Their heads swung around in unison.

"Welcome," said a man in a white collarless button-down, the kind worn by poets or pirates. "Pull up a chair."

I did.

"Introduce yourself."

"I'm River."

"Hi, River," said the man. "Tell us why you're here."

"Um . . ." I swallowed hard. I didn't want a return of the frog. "Well . . . I guess I have issues. Like, I don't think enough about things? And my life is . . . kinda ruined." I stopped. Swallowed again. My mouth was so dry. Why didn't I buy that Boba tea? "And then I . . . I saw the sign. You know, on the building? And, well, I just . . . I need a second chance."

All the people in the circle, most of them about my age except for the Poet/Pirate, did a strange motion, something like a hang-loose, a shaking of the hand back and forth in my direction with the pinky aimed at me and the thumb aimed at themselves.

"That means we feel a connection," explained the Poet/ Pirate. "We're connecting what you're saying to something true inside ourselves." He smiled at me and held my gaze for just long enough to make me a little uncomfortable; then he turned to the kid sitting next to him. This kid was big—shaved head, plaid shirt, thick neck—the kind of kid who looked like he'd steal your lunch money right before hot-wiring your car. "Go on, Mason. You were telling us about what happened this week."

"Okay, so yeah, there I was, like, in the Starbucks after school. Everyone was going, so I figured I'd just go along but I wouldn't get anything. And then everyone was buying Caramel Flan Frappuccinos and they looked so good. But they have like a gajillion calories. And then I see that there's a light Caramel Flan Frappuccino that has only like a hundred and forty calories and zero fat so I get one, and it tastes *exactly* like it has only a hundred and forty calories and zero grams of fat. And I finish it in thirty seconds and I go to order a real one, because now I have the taste for it, and the guy's like *What can I get you?* And I open my mouth to say *A Caramel Flan Frappuccino, dickwad,* but I hear myself say: *A glass of water, please.* It's not like I didn't think about going into the bathroom and puking, but then . . . I didn't. I only made myself throw up once this week. That's not perfect, but I'm pretty proud of that."

"You should be," said the Poet/Pirate. "I know I'm proud of you." He was slight, practically swimming in that collarless shirt, with longish brown hair Penny would have made him trim in the back, a wispy goatee it was unclear he'd fully committed to, and reddish cheeks. He spoke with the hint of a lisp.

How exactly this guy or this group was going to help me get a second chance with Penny I wasn't totally sure, but now I was here, a part of this circle, and I couldn't just stand up and leave.

Counterclockwise, kids gave snapshots of their weeks. Some talked about drugs or alcohol. There was a girl who shoplifted and a boy with a video game addiction. Listening to these kids, I could almost forget about my shattered heart.

Almost.

When the turn came for the kid sitting next to me to speak, he stared at his shoes for a really long time. They were killer kicks: Nike Dunk High SBs in purple and cherry red. I'd never seen this particular color combo. They were limited editions by the looks of them.

He still hadn't said a word. He cracked every knuckle twice and tapped his fingers nervously on his thighs. Nobody rushed him. Time didn't seem to matter. Silence makes me nervous, but there was no way I was going to move to fill it. Finally, he let out a low, slow groan.

"Uuuuuuugggggghhhhhh." And then: "Molly."

The Poet/Pirate nodded.

"Molly," the kid said again, squeezing his eyes tight to keep in the tears. "I. Miss. Molly. I. Miss. Molly. So. Much."

So I wasn't alone. I hadn't wandered into the wrong

place. My sadness, my story, what had brought me here to this room—Penny—it counted. It mattered. I wasn't the only one with a stomped-on heart.

A beautiful girl with long dark hair and light brown skin, pink lipstick and gold hoop earrings, the girl who shoplifted, stood and walked over to the boy in the killer shoes and offered him a Kleenex from her purse. He shooed her away. He was going to hold on to the fiction that he didn't need to cry over Molly the way I'd held on to the rope in that boat.

I wanted to say something like *I feel you, brother,* but I didn't want to speak. Instead I made a fist, stuck out my thumb and pinky and waved my hand back and forth between us.

He looked at me. "You too?"

I nodded.

"Molly?"

I laughed a little. "Well, not *Molly,*" I said. The kid had a dry sense of humor.

"What, then?"

I thought about where to begin. The day I first saw Penny across the courtyard at freshman orientation? The first time I kissed her, at Jonas's party? The first time she let me—

"Coke? Oxy?"

Oh shit. Molly . . . *the drug.* Molly was not a girl. Molly was a drug.

"Adderall?"

I shook my head.

"So what, then?" He eyed me suspiciously. "Whoa . . . not . . . the Big H?"

I shook my head again. More emphatically.

Now he laughed. "I didn't think so. So what is it? Is it . . . weed?"

I nodded, because it was easier than saying I was here for the issues my girlfriend said I had that I didn't fully understand.

And at least I'd actually smoked pot.

Twice.

"Weed?" He laughed again. "Weed," he said like he couldn't believe it.

"Christopher," the Poet/Pirate said. "We can't compare our struggles or our vices to those of our comrades, so we mustn't try. You know this."

"Weed," he cackled.

Everyone was looking at me. Waiting. It was my turn to tell my story.

And that is how I came to attend A Second Chance, on a bleak stretch of midcity Pico, to grapple with my non-existent marijuana addiction, every Saturday night in the spring of my senior year—what should have been the best time of my life.

THREE

Penny didn't show up at school on Monday.

There was only one reasonable explanation for her absence: she stayed home, in bed, sick with regret.

I'd barely made it to school myself. I'd hardly slept, imagining all the ways I might approach Penny when I saw her in the morning, or wondering if I should even approach her at all. Did I want her to see what she'd done to me? How she'd destroyed me? Or was it better to pretend I was fine? That I could face that Monday like any other Monday, with maybe the slightest hint of a swagger, the kind reserved for the guys who believed that the world, and the girls who filled it, were theirs for the taking.

I returned home late on Saturday night. The meeting at A Second Chance didn't let out until eight-thirty, and then everyone hung out a bit out front on the sidewalk, some smoked cigarettes, and before I knew it I'd agreed to bring the snacks the following week.

The Poet/Pirate, whose name turned out to be Everett,

asked me to step back inside for a "chat," during which he asked if I'd been sent to the group or had come voluntarily.

"Voluntarily," I answered.

"That's great. That's big. Recognizing you need the help and taking first steps . . . good for you. We're glad to have you join us." A big smile. Another long stare. "So just how serious is your problem, River?"

"How serious?"

"Yes. If you're in dire shape, in the throes of addiction, this won't be enough. The kids who come here are getting medical help elsewhere, or maybe they've already been through a residential program, and this is a place to come each week and just connect to other kids like them. To share our stories. We live in a vast city, River. As diverse as we are, it's sometimes hard to find people just like us."

Penny said I had issues. That I didn't think about anything. Wouldn't she be pleased if she knew I'd gone straight from that pedal boat to a support group for kids with problems? I was taking action. I was doing something.

I looked Everett in the eye. "This sounds like just what I need."

"Great." He handed me a yellow pamphlet. "We have rules, River, and you're going to need to follow them if you want to continue to come to meetings. Read through this before next week, okay?"

I folded it into quarters and shoved it in my pocket. "Okay."

It took me another two hours to walk home—I probably could have done it in an hour and a half, but I wasn't in a hurry. I was going to fix this. Fix me. And fix us.

At red lights I flipped through Everett's pamphlet. It outlined the sorts of rules you'd expect: Respect the privacy and boundaries of fellow group members. No intimate relationships. What happens at meetings is confidential unless there's concern someone may harm himself or others. Be helpful and supportive. Keep criticism constructive. Tell the truth.

Mom and Leonard were sitting by the fireplace—Mom reading, Leonard going over some blueprints. We couldn't actually light a fire, because we didn't have a chimney, so Mom filled our faux fireplace with candles. She had a gift for taking something simple, or something lacking, and turning it into something special.

"How was the lake?" Leonard asked.

I'm sure they figured Penny and I had gone to dinner afterward, or to the movies, or that we'd gone back to her house, because that was where I spent most of my time. Her house was about four times as big as ours and afforded us the kind of privacy we used to crave. I know they didn't imagine that Penny'd dumped me and that I'd walked all the way home from Echo Park with a brief stop to get support for my addiction to pot.

"Spectacular," I said.

"Nice." Mom looked up from her book for the first time, at me, but I guess I looked unchanged enough that she went back to reading.

"Maybe we'll all go sometime," Leonard said. "Do you think Natalie would like it?"

Natalie, my eight-year-old sister, has a major thing for aquatic mammals. "Natalie would love it. There are turtles, so . . ."

"Say no more."

I spent most of Sunday shut in my room. I didn't want Mom or Leonard or Natalie asking about Penny, because if I didn't have to answer questions about Penny, to my family, she was still my girlfriend.

That brings me to Monday.

Penny picked me up most mornings, but not every morning—school was close enough for me to walk if I skipped a shower—so it didn't raise any suspicion when I left the house on my own.

I hadn't settled on what I'd do when I saw her. My senses were on high alert, my peripheral vision pushed to its extremity. I didn't want to appear like I was looking for her, but I wanted to know exactly where she was, to be aware of her, so I could stay one step ahead of the game at all times.

By lunchtime it was clear she hadn't come to school. Will, who had English lit with her second period, asked me if she was okay.

"Yeah," I said. "Fine."

He didn't ask any more because Will had had his fill of Penny. So had Luke and Maggie. It's not that they begrudged me having a girlfriend, but there was a world that existed beyond our coupled bliss, and they let me know I was welcome to rejoin them in that other world whenever I felt like it.

"Cool." Will returned to his sandwich.

Will and I met the second week of freshman year when his voice hadn't changed and I still wore lame sneakers, Converse mostly. He'd grown up with a kid named Luke, sort of the way I'd grown up with Maggie, and we joined forces to become a foursome, a quadrangle, until Penny came along.

Anyway, as the afternoon wore on, I became convinced that Penny's regret had made her physically ill. I decided I'd go to her house after school with some soup from her favorite deli or maybe flowers, though the latter seemed the less thoughtful and more textbook gesture. To hell with it, I'd bring both.

I asked Maggie for a ride to the deli.

It wasn't that I couldn't walk to Penny's neighborhood, but I was pretty walked out from Saturday.

"You didn't eat lunch?" Maggie asked.

"I did, I just want to get some soup for Penny."

"Of course. I should have figured."

"She's sick. I thought it might be nice to bring her soup."

She took her eyes off the road to study me. "Is everything okay with you guys?"

I pointed to the windshield: Maggie was a pretty lousy driver, she couldn't afford the distraction, and furthermore, I didn't much want her looking at me.

"Everything's fine. Why?"

"Well . . . I sorta heard today that you guys might be on the rocks."

"Who'd you hear that from?"

"Kendall and them."

Like solving a geometric equation, I could see the lines and arrows that connected Kendall to Vanessa and back to Penny.

"Kendall's a dimwit."

"Totally. Anyway, I knew it couldn't be true. Not you and Penny. No way."

Maggie was right. Not Penny and me.

"And anyway, if there *was* trouble with you and Penny, you'd talk to me about it. You'd know that even if I give you a hard time sometimes about Penny, I'm your oldest friend and I just want you to be happy."

"I know. Thanks, Mags."

She dropped me in front of the deli and offered to wait and drive me to Penny's, but I declined.

"Tell her I hope she feels better," she called out as she swerved back into traffic without even a glance over her shoulder.

I went for the quart of chicken soup rather than the pint. That way Penny would have extra to bring in her lunch tomorrow and she'd be able to say to her friends, "River brought me this. Isn't he the best?"

I walked a few blocks out of my way to pick up some flowers at the grocery store. Orange, her favorite color. They weren't anything special, but they'd have to do. By the time I rang her doorbell, my pits were sweat-soaked.

Juana answered. Her face unreadable. "Hi, River."

"Hi, Juana."

"Penelope isn't home."

"She's not?"

"No. She has a doctor visit today. The one for her glasses."

Penny had terrible eyesight. She wore glasses as a little girl and switched to contacts as soon as she was old enough to put them in and take them out herself. Sometimes, when we'd hang around her house, she'd be too lazy to put in her lenses, and she'd wear these thick-framed black glasses. I wouldn't have minded if she always wore those glasses, but she'd been wanting to get corrective eye surgery forever.

"She had the surgery today?" Suddenly my quart of soup and sad orange supermarket flowers felt woefully inadequate.

"No, the doctor is just looking at her eyes again before he can use the lasers."

"Oh." I couldn't help but notice her noticing my sweaty pit stains.

"Do you want to come in? Wait for Penelope?"

"Any idea when she'll be back?"

"Mrs. Brockaway said before dinner. But then she told me she wants dinner early. So I think they'll be home soon."

"Okay."

Juana took my soup, put it in the fridge and put the flowers in a vase on the kitchen island.

"Can I get you anything, River? Something to drink?"

"Thanks, but no, Juana. I'm fine. Really."

She eyed me. I think she could tell I wasn't fine, that something was bothering me beyond my unsightly pit stains. Juana had a soft spot for me. She started at the Brockaways' right around the time I came into Penny's life, and sometimes I thought I was her favorite member of the family, even though I was just an outsider who spent most of my time there. It was a weird spot to be in, and we were both in it.

I went to find Ben in the family room, where I knew he'd be playing video games. That was pretty much all Ben ever did, which might have had something to do with why he was so chubby. I figured sitting with him would be only slightly less awkward than hanging out with Juana while she cooked dinner.

"Penny's not here," Ben said.

"I know. I'm waiting for her to come home."

"You have sweat stains in your armpits."

"I'm aware of that. Thank you."

"Do you want to play FIFA 14?"

"That depends. Do you want to get your ass kicked?"

We played for a while, and he slaughtered me, and then I started getting too anxious to sit still so I went out to the backyard to throw a ball to Nuisance. He was an inspiration, that dog, fetching ball after ball without lagging, never letting his missing leg slow him down. And then suddenly, midfetch: he stopped. Cocked his head. Cocked it a little more. Then he turned around and bolted into the house, and I knew he'd heard the car pull into the driveway.

Penny was home.

Something told me to wait outside, so I sat down on the back steps. I took slow breaths in . . . and out.

She came over and sat down next to me. "River?" She didn't need to say *What are you doing here*, it was in the way she said my name.

"How are your eyes?"

"They're fine, thanks."

"Good. So are you getting the surgery? I don't think I ever told you, but I really like you in your glasses."

"You did tell me you like me in my glasses. Lots of times."

"I did? Good."

"I think you need to go."

"I brought you soup. And flowers."

"Please, River. My mom is inside. And Ben. This is embarrassing."

"I'm going to fix this, Penny. I'm going to be better."

She stood up and walked back into the kitchen. I followed her.

"River, will you stay for dinner?" Juana asked. "I made extra chicken. And the potatoes you like. The crispy ones."

"No, Juana," Penny said. "River is *not* staying for dinner."

"Oh, okay." Juana turned back to the stove. I did love Juana's potatoes. I loved all Juana's cooking.

I gestured to the vase on the island. "Those are the flowers I was talking about."

"I see them. Thank you. That was very nice of you."

We stood and stared at each other. The only sound in

the room was the sound of Juana's potatoes frying on the stove.

"Well, I guess I'll go, then."

"Yes, you should go."

"Good-bye, Juana," I said.

"Good-bye, River. You come back soon."

"Don't worry, I will."

FOUR

It was all over school by the end of the week.

Penny and River broke up.

Most people thought I'd broken up with her, except for the people who really knew me and knew it would never go down like that.

We only had one class together, Penny and me: Spanish 2, which was *muy, muy* awkward. I arrived first on Tuesday and staked out a new seat on the opposite side of the room. Aside from those fifty minutes, from 12:55 to 1:45 each day, I didn't see her at all.

By Friday afternoon I started to feel the weight of a looming Penny-less weekend.

"I should have gotten you a ticket to Tig Notaro tomorrow," Maggie said. We were sitting in a diner sharing an order of fries. Maggie had to fight like a champ to get her share, but she was skilled in holding her own.

"What's a Tig Notaro?"

She looked at me. "River. I've seen like every one of her shows at Largo. You know that."

"I do?"

"Yeah, you do, because I told you about them."

"Oh, right. What does she play again?"

"She's a comedian," Maggie said. "She plays her wit and unbridled humor like a freaking violin. And she has cancer. Get this: she found out right after her mother died *and* her girlfriend left her."

"She sounds like a real riot."

"Trust me." Maggie swiped the final fry. "She's amazing. I would have asked you to go if I had any idea you'd be single by the time the show came around."

I tried to ignore the dig. "I have plans Saturday anyway."

"You do? Really?" She couldn't hide her shock.

"Yeah, I do." Since I couldn't tell her I had to bring the snacks to the support group for my fake marijuana addiction, I said, "I'm going out to dinner with Leonard. Male bonding or whatever. He's pretty much forcing me."

"That's nice." Maggie did a little pouty face at me. Everyone loved Leonard, but Maggie loved him especially because she knew me in the years between when my dad left us and when my mom met Leonard, and let's just say those weren't the golden years for what remained of the Dean family. Mom struggled to balance her job at the nonprofit where she worked on global access to water with raising a boy who was often described, lovingly, as a "major handful." I spent most of my formative afternoons at Maggie's house baking cookies, having tea parties and letting Maggie give me makeovers until Mom could leave the office. Mom and I ate a lot of microwave dinners back then. We didn't have a Juana.

"Maybe I'll see you after," I said.

"Yeah, maybe."

Everyone knows that nobody walks in LA, there's even a song about it—so I probably looked like a vagrant as I wandered along Pico Boulevard early Saturday evening weighed down by grocery bags. I'd picked up brownie bites, veggie chips and kettle corn; then right as I got to the front of the checkout line, I thought of Mason, and ran back to grab a plastic tub of fat-free meringues.

I still hadn't told my family about the breakup; somehow I dreaded telling Natalie the most. Natalie loved Penny because Penny wore dresses and mascara, and Penny tied her hair up in a bun, and she carried this roll-on stick of perfume in her purse that she'd let Natalie try. Mom was your basic grown-up tomboy with a short haircut who never wore anything other than Levi's and sweatshirts except when she took rich people to lunch to ask for money, and then she'd bust out a black pantsuit.

Mom and Leonard really liked Penny, but I was less worried they'd mourn her than I was they'd start to focus unwanted attention on me. Right now I came and went as I pleased without having to account for my whereabouts. They trusted me partly because I had such a trustworthy girlfriend. Ha.

Christopher, of the Molly habit and enviable sneakers, was standing out front with the shoplifter and Mason, the brutish bulimic.

"It's the snack man!" Christopher called when he saw me approaching. "What'd you bring us, snack man?"

I handed over my shopping bags for inspection.

"You know why you got assigned snacks, right?" Mason asked.

"Um, no?"

"'Cause you understand the munchies."

"You got the experience," added the girl. "You got, like, the institutional knowledge."

"And? How'd I do?"

She peered into the bags again. "I give you a C-plus."

"A C-plus? That's all?"

"Well, you got sweet and savory, yes. And you have soft and crunchy. You get bonus points for the fat-free option. But you don't have anything crispy. Nothing fresh. And let's not even get started on how you didn't bring anything to drink. With all this sodium?" She waved a finger with a long pink-painted nail at me. "Tsk. Tsk."

"I'm new. Go easy on me."

She looked me up and down. "Okay. B-minus."

"Grade inflation." Christopher blew out a final plume of smoke and stubbed out his cigarette on the sole of his gorgeous shoe.

"Don't be mad, Christopher," she said. "You're still the reigning snack champ. But that's only 'cause you're rich as hell." She looked at me. "Club kid. Club drugs. You know the type. He brings those individually wrapped nut bars that cost two bucks each. Those are sick."

Everett opened the door to the meeting room. He was wearing a green T-shirt with an elephant on the front.

"Hello, Mason. Christopher. Daphne." He nodded at me. "River, I'm glad you came back."

"Well, I had to bring the snacks, so . . ."

"It takes courage to come here."

"Or a consent decree," muttered Daphne.

"Yes," he said. "Sometimes the terms of one's arrest and restitution dictate that the defendant attend a counseling program, but it's our goal that we all come here because we want to, not because we have to."

"I'm just messing with you, Everett," she said, shoving him playfully. "You know I live for this."

He let us inside and we all unfolded chairs and set up a circle. A quiet fell naturally over the group, and then Everett began a call and response.

"Here," he said.

"Is where we belong," the group chanted.

"This."

"Is where change begins."

"Now."

"Is the time."

I'd chosen my seat in the circle so that I'd share last, but Everett pulled a fast one, switching the direction to clockwise.

I told everyone I'd had a hard week, which triggered many of those hand gestures. I said I'd fought for what

I wanted (Penny, which they interpreted to mean my sobriety) but that I'd lost (Penny, which they interpreted to mean I'd gotten high). I said I wanted to get better, to *be* better. I said I wanted to think about things more.

"Don't be too hard on yourself," Everett said.

"Yeah," Daphne added. "If you wanna be hard on yourself, be hard on yourself for bringing mediocre snack foods."

This kid with a lazy eye talked next about how he stole a six-pack from his stepmother and blamed it on his sister.

"She's only fourteen and she doesn't drink," he said. "But my stepmother hates her and is always looking for an excuse to punish her, so I knew she'd believe me . . . or at least pretend to. I did feel kinda bad about it, though. My sister was, like, crying for hours because she had to miss her friend's party."

I couldn't imagine making Natalie cry. Ever hurting her on purpose. If I wanted to dodge blame for something, Natalie would be the last person in the world I'd throw under the bus. But I knew I was in a much different place than most of the people in this room. That my issues, whatever they were, paled in comparison.

This girl Bree spoke about eating only green leafy vegetables for three days straight. Daphne told us she'd put a mascara in her pocket but then returned it to the shelf before leaving the store. And Christopher dreamed of feeling the same kind of euphoria without the drugs.

Despite all the talking—So. Much. Talking.—the meeting quieted something inside me. Outside this room, everything in my life reminded me of Penny, and I couldn't catch my breath without breathing in more of her. Even though I'd stumbled into A Second Chance because of her, she felt far away from that circle. I spent my time in the room thinking about people other than Penny; I could even start to see her in my rearview mirror.

Here was where I belonged. *This* was where change began.

The meeting ended before I felt ready for it to. It was Saturday night at eight o'clock and one of my best friends was off listening to a comedian with cancer and I didn't know where the other two were because I'd become a lousy friend. I had nowhere to go and nothing to do.

Out on the sidewalk Everett asked, "So we'll see you next week, even though you're relieved of snack duty?"

I nodded. I wanted to come back. Penny was onto something when she said I didn't think about things. Now I was working on that.

I watched him and most of the kids walk away, toward their own cars or cars that waited for them out front. Christopher lit another cigarette and Daphne hung back, so I did too, and then it occurred to me that maybe there was something going on between them and I was just a third wheel.

She tugged on one of her large hoop earrings and narrowed her eyes at me. "So why are you really here, River? What's your real story?"

I felt my face go bright red. It was a curse of my partial Nordic heritage. One of the many unwelcome gifts my father left me along with fatherlessness. And my stupid first name.

"Awww," she said. "I made you blush."

"Nah." Christopher took a deep drag from his cigarette. "He just knows in his heart that an addiction to weed is wicked embarrassing."

"Kids don't usually come here because it's how they want to spend a Saturday night," Daphne said. "So what's your story? Your parents find your stash? You get caught dealing at school? You got a lady who likes you better when you're straight?"

"I'm just . . . here because I want to be here," I said.

"Yeah, sure."

"What?"

"That reeks of bullshit," Daphne said. She stared at me long and hard. Christopher chuckled. "But you do look like you're hurting. I can see that. It's in your eyes."

I brought my hand up and rubbed my forehead, shielding my face.

"The problem isn't *that* you need weed, River," she said. "It's *why* you need weed. So why? Why do you need weed?"

I wished I smoked cigarettes like Christopher so I could take a long, thoughtful drag off one. Instead I just stared at the sidewalk and thought of Penny. "I guess it's what made my life feel full. And without it . . ."

"You're empty."

"Well, thanks for the Hallmark memories, guys," Christopher said. "I'm outta here."

"Right. Me too." I turned and started walking west. I

figured Largo wasn't too far out of the way—maybe I'd wait for the Tig Notaro show to get out and hitch a ride home with Maggie. Or maybe I'd get lucky and there'd still be tickets left. I could have used a good laugh.

Daphne called out after me. "Yo, River! You . . . *walking?*"

"Yep."

"But nobody walks in LA!"

"Nobody but me."

There weren't any tickets left, and the bouncer was unmoved by how my best friend was inside and I needed a laugh, so I waited across the street at a bus stop for the show to get out. Penny was right. I had never once, in all my seventeen years in Los Angeles, taken a single bus. And waiting for Maggie helped illustrate why—I sat in that bus stop for forty-five minutes and no bus ever came.

When the crowd started spilling out onto the sidewalk, I searched for her. It was a big crowd, so I stood up on the bench to get a better view, and that was when I spied them, shoulder to shoulder, still smiling at some joke: Maggie, Will and Luke.

I didn't call out to them. I'm not totally sure why it bothered me that Maggie never mentioned they were all going to the show. They usually did things together while I spent my time with Penny. But now I'd lost Penny and it was starting to sink in that I'd lost my connection to my friends too. I'd ruined everything.

I watched them climb into Will's car—he'd scored the rock star spot out front because Will always had luck on his side—and I watched them drive away.

I sat back down on the bench in the bus stop. I had no idea if the bus that hadn't arrived yet would take me anywhere near where I lived, but I gave it another fifteen minutes and when it still hadn't come, I took out my phone and dialed my mom.

I'm not going to lie—I thought about calling Penny. After everything we'd been through together, how could she have left me sitting alone at a bus stop at the corner of La Cienega and Oakwood at ten o'clock at night? But I didn't call because I wanted her to think I was out somewhere having fun, out forgetting her, maybe even with another girl.

"Hi, honey."

"Hi, Mom."

"You okay?"

"Yeah, um, I sorta need a ride."

"Where's Penny?"

"Long story. Can you just come get me?"

"Of course."

FiVE

Mom's way of dealing with what I told her on the ride home was to make me pancakes for breakfast. The kind where she has to separate the eggs and beat the whites, not the kind from a mix.

"Oooo, homemade pancakes," Leonard said. "What's the occasion?"

"It's okay, Leonard. You don't have to pretend you don't know. I know Mom told you, and I'm fine with that. In fact I'm fine all around."

"Mom told Dad what?" Natalie asked.

I looked at her. She had Leonard's dark hair and the biggest brown eyes you've ever seen. No Nordic curse for this one. She was still in her striped pajamas with the feet. I envied her pajamas. It was so much simpler being eight.

"Well, the thing is, Nat," I said, and I put my hand on hers. "Penny and I broke up."

Her hand flew up to cover her mouth. "Oh no!" Quick as a flash her big eyes filled with tears. "No! No, no, no!"

"It's okay, kid. Really. I'm okay. See?" I took her hand back and put it on my forehead. "No fever." I took her fingers and poked myself in the chest with them. "No pain." I smiled at her, hoping I'd made it look genuine. "I'm shipshape."

"But . . . Penny was so nice. Penny was so pretty."

"Yes, Penny was both of those things. And she still is, actually."

"Well, she's not nice if she broke up with you."

"How do you know I didn't break up with her?"

She looked at me like I was an utter idiot. "Because you would never."

"True."

We ate our pancakes and I did the dishes and Natalie disappeared into her room. I had loads of homework to do—I'd let it pile up last week, getting extensions and basically treating myself like an invalid. Now the mountain in front of me seemed totally unscalable. All I wanted to do was to crawl back into bed, which I did. I slept for another two hours.

When I woke I forced myself to sit at my desk and open up my precalc textbook, but the numbers and symbols just swarmed in front of my eyes, unreadable as hieroglyphics. All my college applications were in, I'd earned my senior slide, but I couldn't flat-out ignore my homework.

A light knock that could only have been delivered by a hand as small as Natalie's.

"Come in."

She slipped a folded piece of red construction paper underneath the door. I opened up her card. She'd used glitter, which got all over my hands and spilled out onto the floor.

Dear River Dean—
Would you like to go out to ice cream with me today?
Check the yes box for yes. Or the no box for no.
Your sister,
Natalie Marks

That we had different last names, and different fathers, was a major obsession of Natalie's. It didn't matter how many times I told her I couldn't possibly adore her any more. That I felt happy for her that she had Leonard and not my narcissistic asshole as a father. Okay, so maybe I didn't say *narcissistic asshole*, I probably said something like *jerk*. Anyway, she'd always had a hard time accepting our family situation and begged me to change my name.

"Don't you like the sound of River Anthony Marks?" she'd ask.

"Sure, Nat. But I'm used to my name."

"Why?" A favorite question of hers.

"Because it's who I am," I'd say.

"I think you're more of a River Marks than a River Dean."

Now we walked the extra distance to the new gourmet ice cream shop. Ice cream after pancakes seemed a little like overkill, but how could I turn down a glittery invitation, especially when it gave me such a good excuse to close my precalc textbook?

The vibe of the place was old-school soda fountain, and we took two stools at the counter, where a guy in a bow tie and paper hat took our order.

Natalie reached into the little purse she'd brought along. "Are you planning on picking up the check today?"

"No way. I'm just getting out my notebook."

"Why?"

"Because, silly, we have to take notes."

"On what?"

"On how you can get Penny back."

How much did I love this kid? Nobody else, not one other person in my life, held out any hope for Penny and me.

I thought for a minute. "I brought her soup," I told Natalie. "Her favorite soup from her favorite deli. A whole quart of it. I have no idea if she ever drank it."

"Girls don't like soup. They like pretty stuff."

"I also bought her flowers."

She took out her pencil and wrote *flowers* in her notebook and then put a little box and a check next to it.

"Flowers. That's much better." She tapped the pencil to her chin. "What about poetry?"

"What about it?"

"Does Penny like poetry?"

Does Penny like poetry? We'd done a poetry unit last year in our AP English class. Most of what we read was bullshit. Honestly, I can hardly remember anything except for this poem about a guy out driving at night who finds a dead deer by the side of the road. I remember Penny being really bummed about how the guy pushed the deer over the edge of a cliff at the end. She was a total sucker for animals, especially sick or vulnerable ones, which was how she wound up with a three-legged dog. Anyway, I was pretty sure the key to winning Penny back didn't have anything to do with a dead deer.

"Maybe you could write her a poem?"

"Hmmmm. I don't think so, Nat."

She placed an X in the box next to *poetry*.

"Girls like jewelry."

"I know. I've seen all the same movies you have and then some. Plus I gave Penny plenty of jewelry over the last two years."

"Did you ever give her anything with diamonds in it?"

"No."

"Why?"

"Because I'm not a gajillionaire."

"I have some money in my piggy bank."

"Listen, Nat." I took my spoon and tried to dip it into her ice cream, but she blocked me with her spoon like an expert fencer. "I don't need to buy Penny stuff. That's not what this is about. And it's not what it should be about for you when you're old enough to fall in love."

"I am old enough!"

"Fine, but just don't pick your boyfriend based on what he buys you."

She thought this over. "Okay."

"Penny broke up with me because . . . well, because . . ." I still didn't have a good enough answer to this. "Well, she said I have issues and that I don't think enough about things."

"That's weird."

"It is weird, isn't it? But I'm working on it."

We sat and finished our ice creams in silence. Natalie licked her spoon clean and as much of the inside of the cup as she could get to.

"I liked Penny," she said.

"Me too."

"It's not fair that I didn't get a chance to say good-bye to her."

That was when I got my idea. The kid wanted the chance to say good-bye to Penny, and what kind of brother would I be if I didn't help the kid get what she wanted? I'd bring her to Penny's house.

We went on Wednesday after school. I told Mom I'd pick up Natalie from her gymnastics class.

"Really?"

"Yes."

"But how?"

"I'll get Maggie to drive me."

Mom eyed me. Much as she adored Maggie, we shared the same opinion about her driving.

"Fine, I'll get Will or Luke to do it."

"Okay. You're sure about this?"

"Yes, Mom. Totally sure."

"Because she's eight years old. If you forget her at her gymnastics class, those scars won't heal."

"Mom. I'm not going to forget Natalie. If there's anyone who understands about those scars, it's probably me."

"Honey. I just meant that sometimes you get . . . distracted."

This was precisely why I didn't want to tell her about Penny and me breaking up. She thought I couldn't be trusted to do anything on my own.

I asked Will to drive me over lunch.

"So . . . you're trying to use your adorable little sister to get to Penny."

"No. Natalie just wanted a chance to say good-bye to her."

"You're shameless."

I would never *use* Natalie, but Penny cared about her. There was no way she'd dare be rude and cold to me in front of Natalie. And she always told me she admired what a good big brother I was, so, yes, I thought maybe when she saw me with my sister, she'd remember one of the things about me that made me worth loving. But I couldn't admit any of this to Will.

"Are you going to ask Penny if it's okay to come by?"

"No."

"But aren't you going to see her next period in Spanish?"

"Will, are you going to give me the ride or not?"

"I'm not sure."

"What aren't you sure about?"

"If I want to aid and abet you in making an ass of yourself."

He finally agreed to do it, and we picked Natalie up right on time. She was wearing this pink velvet leotard, with her hair in pigtails. It was like she'd dressed for her starring role in the smash hit *Win Back Penny's Love*.

Natalie jumped on Will's back and he rode her out to his car, galloping and zigzagging while she laughed and clutched his neck.

"How are you guys going to get home?" he asked as we idled in front of Penny's house.

"We'll walk."

"No way. I'm not walking home," Natalie said. "No way."

"We'll figure it out."

"I can wait here if you want," Will offered. "You should make it quick anyway."

We climbed out of the car and I leaned back into the passenger window. "It's okay, Will. I hereby relieve you of your chauffeuring duties. Carry on."

He gave me a disapproving look. "Suit yourself."

Juana answered the door again, but this time I could read her face. She knew Penny and I were over, and she knew it probably wasn't a good thing that I was standing on the doorstep with my pigtailed little sister.

"Hello, River." She leaned down a little bit and managed a smile at Natalie. "Hello, princess. You must be Natalie."

"I am."

She stuck out her hand and Natalie took it. "I've heard so much about you. It's nice to put such a cute face together with the name."

Natalie looked at me. Not sure what to do or say next. Juana hadn't invited us in.

"Um," Natalie said. "We've come to see Penny."

"Is she . . . expecting you?"

"No," Natalie said. "It's a surprise."

Juana thought it over for a minute, but what were her options? She couldn't just turn us away. Natalie was sweet and cute, yes, but also, Juana and I shared the role of almost-family to the Brockaways. We were like almost-cousins.

"Penelope!" she called. "You have visitors!"

She led us into the kitchen, put out a plate of cookies and poured us glasses of milk. She knew just what I liked, but I held back. I didn't want Penny to find me with a milk mustache.

Penny went right to Natalie and gave her a big hug, swinging her back and forth. She kissed the top of Natalie's head.

"Hiya, Natty." Penny put her back down. "Look at you. You look ready for the Olympics!"

"I wish you hadn't broken up with River."

Penny shot me a look. I shrugged, like: *I swear I didn't put her up to this.*

"Listen, Nat," Penny said. "You wanna come upstairs for a minute? I have a new perfume I think you're gonna love."

Natalie put down her cookie and took Penny by the

hand. I couldn't decide if I should feel betrayed or in awe. I had no idea what the kid's end game was.

I wolfed down two cookies and chugged my glass of milk, wiping my mouth and waving off Juana's offer of more.

She cleared my plate and glass. "She's sweet, your sister."

"Yeah, I know. She's a good one." I could tell Juana wanted to say something else. Probably she wanted to yell at me to run and take my dignity with me.

"She's lucky to have a brother like you. Nobody will ever know you in the same way you two know each other."

I'd heard something like this before. It was one of the things adults liked to say, along with telling me it wasn't my fault that my father left me.

"My brother and I, we grew up side by side working in my grandmother's restaurant. To this day we can make a whole meal without ever speaking a word to each other."

"You should open your own restaurant, Juana. You're an amazing cook."

She wiped the counter in front of me even though I'd been careful not to make a mess. "That would be something."

"Potatoes could be your signature dish."

"I can do so much more, River." She leaned closer and dropped her voice. "But the Brockaways? They want simple food. Nothing interesting. No spice."

Natalie burst into the kitchen with a small round container in the palm of her hand. "Look, River! Penny had an extra silver eye shadow she gave me for keeps!"

"I told her it's only for dress-up. No wearing it out of the house, right?" Penny looked at Natalie.

Natalie nodded. "Right."

Penny gave her another hug. "Thanks so much for coming by. It really meant a lot to me."

"Thanks for the eye shadow. And the perfume." Natalie leaned into me and held out her forearm. "Smell me, River."

She smelled like Penny.

I put my arm around Natalie's shoulder and we stood facing Penny by the kitchen island while Juana washed dishes in the sink.

"Well . . . good-bye." Penny took her hair out of its bun and started to tie it up again. It was one of her nervous tics, redoing her already perfectly done hair.

"We need a ride home," Natalie said.

I squeezed her shoulder. "No, no. It's okay, we'll walk."

Natalie took a step away from me and folded her arms across her chest. "I told you I'm not walking, and I'm not. I'm *not* walking home."

Penny watched us.

I pulled my phone out of my pocket. "I can call Maggie or one of those guys. Luke has practice, and Will already drove us here, so it's probably too much to make him come back again, especially at this time of day, but maybe Maggie can—"

"Juana," Penny said, staring me down. "Can you please drive River and Natalie home?"

Juana turned off the faucet and wiped her hands on a dish towel.

"I have to make dinner, and your mother, she said—"

"Just do it, Juana." And then Penny added, "Please."

"Okay, if you really need—"

"Thank you."

Penny turned and walked out of the room.

We followed Juana down the driveway past Penny's SUV and across the street to a dark green Toyota Camry, an old one, with a smashed-in front left bumper and a sticker on the rear fender for a radio station I'd never listened to.

Juana lived with the Brockaways except for on the weekends. I'd had no idea she had a car, or where she went when she wasn't here, but of course she had a car, because this was Los Angeles.

"Thanks for doing this for us," I said as Natalie hopped in the backseat. "Really, we appreciate it."

"It's okay," Juana said. "You're a nice boy, River."

I told her where our house was and which streets I'd avoid considering it was rush hour.

I turned to face Natalie. "So how'd it go upstairs?"

"Fine. She told me she was sorry. And that she'd miss seeing a lot of me but that we could still be friends."

"Well, that's nice of her."

"And I told her that she's wrong about you."

"What do you mean?"

"Well, I told her that she's wrong when she says that

you don't think about stuff, because you do. You do think about stuff. I know you do."

We drove in silence with the radio turned down low. A Spanish-language station. Probably the one on the bumper sticker. I watched as the plastic religious figure that hung from the rearview mirror swung back and forth as we stopped and started through evening traffic.

When we pulled up in front of our house I thanked Juana again. "I know driving me around really isn't your job. I'm sorry Penny made you take me."

She put a hand on my cheek. "Like I said, you're a nice boy, River. You have a kind heart. I know this about you."

As Natalie climbed out from the backseat, she spied the dangling plastic figure. She reached over and touched him.

"Who's this?" she asked Juana.

"This is St. Jude."

"Who's St. Jude?"

"He's a saint. The patron saint of lost causes."

SiX

By week three at A Second Chance it was no longer possible for me to be vague about my problem with weed.

Time to get down and dirty.

During Bree's turn she put her face in her hands and wept, her body gently shaking. Nobody said anything; we just sat by and let her feel her sadness. Daphne rubbed her back. Usually when people cry in front of me it makes me super uncomfortable, or "uncunchterble," like Natalie used to say, and I feel embarrassed for the person doing the crying and I just want to do something to make it stop and put us both out of our misery. I did feel pretty uncunchterble at first, but as it went on and on I was able to just feel for her.

Daphne was up next.

"So usually I shop at Ralphs or the Vallarta, or if I can get a ride or I got the car, we go to Costco. But we needed ziplock bags because we were out and I got four lunches to make each day not including my own, so I walked to the little grocery a few blocks away. The store's got nothing you want, and the guy who runs the place is rude, so I don't go there on principle, but it was night, and I had to make lunches for the next day, and so I go there and he's only got some crap brand with like eighteen bags in the box and I'm all: that's barely gonna get me through one day of lunches. And the box costs four ninety-nine. That's like twenty-eight cents *each bag*. I got enough in my wallet to buy him outta his entire supply of crap ziplock bags. But I just think it'd be so much easier to slip the box into my purse and leave. It would feel *good,* even. To not have to talk to the dick who runs the shop. Not transact with him. But . . . I didn't. I bought two boxes. They lasted me three days."

Everett broke the silence that followed. "Wonderful."

"Wonderful?" Christopher looked at Everett. "Wonderful? Really?"

"Do you have something you want to say, Christopher?"

"Yeah. She—"

"Don't say *she*. Look at Daphne and address her directly, please."

Christopher swiveled in his chair to face Daphne. "That story. It makes you out to be the hero. Like it was some noble act to pay for the overpriced bags. If you didn't want to pay for them, you could have just gone someplace else. And maybe this guy has five kids of his own at home, and they need to eat lunch too, and that's why he tacks a little extra onto the price of his plastic bags. Did you ever think of that?"

She stared back at him.

I must have had the wrong idea about them. Not that I was any relationship expert, but I was pretty sure it wasn't a good idea to talk like that to the girl you're into.

She took a pink lip gloss out of the pocket of her sweatshirt and put it on. I wondered what Penny would have looked like in that lip gloss, because on Daphne it looked kind of amazing. "Yeah, actually, I think you make a good point, Christopher."

Or . . . maybe they did like each other.

"My problem is my problem and I can't go through life thinking I'm doing someone a favor by paying for things. And yeah, hard as it is for me to imagine that guy, like, *procreating,* he probably does have kids at home and he probably does have to fix them lunch." Daphne screwed the top back on her lip gloss and rubbed her lips together. "The funny thing is, most of the other stuff I've ever stolen or thought about stealing was stupid. Like it was something I didn't *need,* and something I didn't even *want.* Once I stole a little porcelain horse. I stole a Zippo lighter and I don't smoke. How I got arrested was I stole a scarf from Macy's downtown. A wool scarf. This is Southern California. I don't *need* a wool scarf." She sighed. "I don't even know what I'm doing half the time."

Hand gestures all around. *We connect what you're saying to something true inside ourselves.*

"So . . . *why?*" I asked.

Daphne looked at me.

"*Why* do you do it? That's what's important, right? The *why* of it?"

"Because I'm sick and tired of having to work so hard all the time while other people just get stuff handed to them. I'm not saying I deserve more than anyone else, I'm just saying I'm smart, okay? And I'm, like, really competent. I'm good at stuff. And I can't have what I want . . . or do what I want, and . . ." She sighed. "Forget it. I know how this sounds."

"It sounds complicated," I said.

She smiled at me. "Yeah. It's complicated."

"So, River." Everett turned to face me. "What's your week been like? What are you doing to stay clean? What are the moments that are hardest for you? What do you miss about getting high, or do you even miss it at all? What's your *why*?"

I took this as Everett's not-so-subtle invitation for me to step up my game. Most of the kids in the group weren't especially articulate, and sometimes they didn't say much at all, so I knew I didn't have to go on at length, but I did have to say something about fighting my addiction.

I thought about the two times I'd smoked weed. The first was at a party. Penny was out of town and I didn't even want to go because parties weren't nearly as much fun without her, half the fun was finding a place to be alone and get her out of as many layers of clothing as she'd let me, but anyway, I went. It was the beginning of junior year and the party was at this kid's house whose dad was a big-time movie producer.

I was with Maggie, Luke and Will. We were hanging out around a fire pit near the pool just talking and some other people came over and lit up a joint. They passed it around and I took it.

It didn't feel like a big deal. I didn't think: *I am about to do illegal drugs for the first time.* I just took a hit, and coughed, and passed it to Maggie and when it came back around to me, I took another hit.

The world didn't go psychedelic or fish-eye-lensed. I just laughed a little more, because everything struck me as a little bit funnier. I did have a moment looking at Maggie, Luke and Will where I thought: *I love these guys. I'm lucky to have them as friends. They bring joy into my life. They support me and stand by me and they're always there for me when I need them.* But of course I didn't say that out loud because who says stuff like that?

The second time wasn't quite as rosy.

We were at the beach. Again, Penny wasn't there. When I'd told her I'd smoked pot at the party she'd been pretty disapproving. Penny was sort of a prude, and I don't say that only because we never had sex; I say it because she was cautious. She made her decisions carefully—something I didn't like thinking about considering her decision about me—and she hated being out of control.

Luke's sister Erica had come home for winter break from college with a significant stash, which Luke promptly pilfered along with some rolling papers. None of us knew how to roll a joint and it was windy so the scene was pretty comical, but we managed. The beach was empty and we climbed up a lifeguard tower and sat with our legs dangling down and passed the joint. I guess I thought if I smoked more I'd laugh a little more and maybe even get hit by another one of those waves of love and appreciation.

Nope.

The world kind of went off track, like a film where the sound doesn't quite keep up, and time didn't make sense anymore. I remember looking at my watch and thinking: *How much time is going by, how much time is going by?* Only, apparently I wasn't thinking it, I was saying it, over and over again until Maggie threw cold water in my face, which only made things worse because then I started thinking, *Why is she throwing water at me—I thought we were friends.*

I didn't tell Penny about that time at the beach, and I hadn't smoked pot since.

"I didn't like what it was doing to me," I heard myself say.

"Mmmmmm." Everett closed his eyes and nodded.

"And . . . and . . . It was like I was operating outside myself, you know, out of sync with everything. So I stopped."

"That's it?" Christopher asked. "You just quit? No problemo?"

"Oh, there was a problemo."

Addicts don't just walk away without a fight. If they did, they probably weren't addicts in the first place. This much I knew from the Say No to Drugs assemblies. So I tried imagining needing something so badly I couldn't quit it.

I imagined Penny.

"I couldn't stop," I went on. "It became the most important thing in my life. It was all I thought about first thing in the morning. All I thought about all day long. When can I get high? My whole life became about: When can I get high again? I stopped hanging out with my friends. And then . . . my girlfriend broke up with me."

I had to take a moment. The fake stuff came naturally, but the true statement, *my girlfriend broke up with me,* was hard to say out loud.

"It does all come with a hefty price tag, don't it?" Mason stared at me in a way that was less: *I connect what you're saying to something true inside myself,* and more: *I could harm you physically without breaking a sweat.*

"Honestly, without her . . . I feel pretty lost," I said. "And I don't know how to put her behind me."

"Is that how you like it, River? With the girl behind you?" Mason doubled over with laughter, slapping himself on the shoulder because there was no one with whom he could share a high five.

"Mason," Everett said.

"What?"

"It doesn't sound like you're listening. Or taking River seriously."

"Oh, I'm listening. I'm listening real good. But it's pretty hard to take River seriously. I mean—look at him."

So, of course, everyone did. My face burned Nordic red.

Everett studied me. "He's struggling, Mason. Just like you. Just like all of us."

"So . . ." Daphne caught my eye. "The weed was just filling a hole you already had. That's your why. You let it be everything so you didn't have to pay attention to what you're missing."

"Maybe." Why had I made Penny my everything? What was I missing? I had a good shot at a great college. A family who loved me. Friends who put up with me even when I disappeared. Sure, I had a father who'd abandoned me, but I tried not to dwell on that. I was a reasonably good-looking white male from the Westside of Los Angeles. I'd pretty much won the lottery.

"Or maybe," I said, "I wasn't really missing anything. Maybe . . . I'm just weak."

"Sorry I was such a dick," Mason said to me outside afterward. "I can be that way sometimes, and I don't even know why. It's like I have two personalities or something. Good Mason and Bad Mason. I never know who's out ahead." He stuck out his hand. "Accept my apology?"

"Sure."

"And I'm sorry your lady broke your heart."

"Yeah," Daphne added. "That hurts."

"Dude," Christopher said. "You should embrace your freedom. Girls are nothing but trouble."

"Wow," Daphne said. "How do you not have a girl-friend? With all that sweet, romantic talk."

"So what you're saying is: you wanna be my girlfriend?"

"No thank you, Christopher. You got too many issues."

"Ha!"

She waved her hand in his face. "And I don't have time."

"You don't have time for a boyfriend?" I asked. This struck me as a bullshit excuse. Something along the lines of *It's not you, it's me* or *I just think we're better as friends* or *You don't think enough about things.*

"Look, I take care of my brothers and sisters all week long. Morning and night. And then I come here Saturdays, because, you know, I have to. So when do you figure I have time for a relationship?"

Christopher finished his cigarette and reached into his pocket for his car keys. "Well, it's been real, suckers, but I'm all shared out."

Mason checked his phone. "Aw . . . balls."

"What?" Christopher asked.

"My friend was supposed to pick me up but he's bailing. Can you give me a ride home?"

"Depends. Where do you live?"

"Culver City."

Culver City wasn't all that far from my house. I quickly weighed the embarrassment of getting shot down against a five-mile walk alone in the dark.

"I live in Rancho Park," I added. "I could kinda use a ride too."

Christopher threw his arms out. "Anyone else? Apparently I am now a taxi service. Daphne? Do you need a ride?"

"Nah," she said. "I'm gonna take the bus."

"The bus?" I asked. "Really? But nobody takes the bus in LA."

"White people don't," she said. "Mexicans do."

I felt that Nordic curse rise in my cheeks. Why was I such a clueless asshole?

"I mean . . . what I meant . . . I meant to say . . ."

"You meant to say that you don't ride the bus and neither do your friends because you all have cars."

"No . . . I meant . . ."

"River. Untangle your panties, will you?"

"C'mon." Christopher motioned to Daphne. "I'll drive you home too."

"Do you even know where I live?"

"No."

"Boyle Heights."

"Okay."

"Do you know where that is?"

"Not exactly."

"It's east of downtown. Like, the exact opposite direction from where you're going."

"So?" He tossed his keys up and caught them in midair. "That's why God invented freeways."

SEVEN

Right before we got to where the 10 hits the 110 we four very different people realized that we shared something in common: we were super hungry.

They could say what they wanted about the snacks I'd brought the week before, but at least I'd done better than Bree. Flaxseed chips? Seaweed? Come on.

In all my life, I'd only been to downtown Los Angeles maybe a dozen times, when I'd let Mom drag me to the theater to see *Peter Pan* or *Mary Poppins,* the kind of huge spectacle I couldn't fully appreciate and we couldn't really afford. Mom had groomed Natalie to be her next-generation theater date, and Natalie was doing a much better job in that role than I ever did.

I had no idea where we should go, but the others decided that Philippe's was the perfect spot.

"Who doesn't love a French dip?" Christopher asked as he zipped his Audi A5 through the quiet downtown streets.

The place was packed. Old people. Young people. Big

Chinese families. Guys in jumpsuits with Department of Water and Power patches above their hearts. Cowboy hats and beanies. T-shirts and ties.

As we stood in line to place our orders, Mason must have picked up on my unease about bringing a bulimic into a restaurant that reeked of animal fat.

"I can eat a sandwich," he said slowly as if English wasn't my first language. "I just can't eat five of them."

"Got it."

We collected our order—four French dips, coleslaw, drinks—and we settled into a booth with an old wooden table into which people had carved their initials and some moron had drawn a dick and balls in black Sharpie.

I had a strange flash sitting in that booth with Christopher, Mason and Daphne, imagining this as some upside-down alternate version of my other life, where I might be in a similar booth far west of here with Will, Luke and Maggie. I guessed Daphne would play Maggie in that version, though they looked so different. Maggie was tall and thin with shoulder-length light brown hair she usually tucked behind her ears, and braces at seventeen, her third round, because she was born with the world's most crooked teeth. It was hard for me to *see* Maggie because she'd been my friend since I was two, but everything about Daphne was new to me. She had a small ring in her nose and a tattoo—roses on the vine that wound around her wrist—and her curly hair and eyes were the same shiny black. She had a round face and skin that looked soft. She was quick to smile, and when she did, she went for broke.

Looking at Daphne carefully and imagining her as Maggie led to comparing her to Penny, because all roads led me back to Penny.

Penny's hair was curly too, but it was reddish. She was pale-skinned and covered in freckles that multiplied in summertime and diminished in winter. Her eyes were green. Her lips were thin, never glossed in pink like Daphne's.

"What are you looking at?" Daphne asked.

"Nothing!" I said.

"Really? 'Cause it kinda looked like you were checking me out."

"No, I was—"

"You haven't even touched your sandwich."

I glanced down at my tray. She was right.

Mason and Christopher were staring at me like I was a total bonehead with no game at all. I wanted to explain that I wasn't into Daphne because I was hopelessly in love with Penny, and anyway it was sort of obvious that Daphne and Christopher were into each other, but that would have just made everything even more awkward, so I just picked up my French dip and took a bite. It was delicious.

Christopher had finished his and was itching to go outside for a cigarette. Mason offered to go with him.

"To keep myself from ordering cheesecake," he said. "An entire cheesecake."

Daphne and I sat facing each other, but I could hardly look at her now that I'd been busted for staring.

"So you really weren't checking me out?" she asked.

"Nope."

"Hmmmm."

"What?"

"Usually I know when guys are looking at me *that* way. Because, not to brag or anything, but it sort of happens a lot."

She watched me try to hide my embarrassment by stuffing my face with my sandwich.

"So what kind of name is River, anyway?"

I took a long drink from my Coke. "You mean, who names their kid River? I assume you aren't asking about my country of origin."

"Right. How'd you wind up with a stupid name like River? That's what I'm asking."

"My dad. He wanted something different. Unforgettable. Which is pretty ironic considering he went on to basically forget about me."

"He left?"

"Yep."

"Like, went out for a pack of smokes and never came back kind of left?"

"Close."

"Ouch."

"Yeah."

"I think there's two kinds of men." She fixed those black, shining eyes on me. "The stayers and the leavers. My dad? He's a stayer. I got lucky like that. Five kids and two jobs he works sixty hours a week, mostly on overnight shifts, but he still comes home in the mornings. Your dad?

He's a leaver. That's just who he is. And that's about him. Not you."

I'd heard every single version there was of how I wasn't the reason my dad left—from Mom, Leonard, my friends, a therapist I was forced to see briefly with permanently smudged glasses and an office that smelled like patchouli. Daphne wasn't going to shed any new light on the shitty dad card I'd been dealt.

"Is he a deadbeat?" she asked.

"No, actually. His checks come on time. My mom never even had to fight about it because he offered more than any court would have ordered him to pay. He thinks he can buy a clean conscience."

Sometimes I thought it would have been better if he *had* gone out for a pack of smokes and never returned. Then I could have invented my own narrative about what happened to him—he was kidnapped, he was a secret agent for the government called on a special mission, he'd suffered amnesia and lived a new life with a new family, but every now and then found himself dreaming of a little blond boy with sad blue eyes, and when he woke he couldn't shake the feeling that this boy was real.

But thanks to the powers of modern technology, there was no mystery about Thaddeus Dean. I could Google him. I could look at pictures of him. I could watch videos of him giving speeches with a little microphone attached to his headset like he was the captain of the *Millennium Falcon*.

Most of my sandwich sat untouched. I wasn't all that hungry anymore.

"Well, at least he sends money," Daphne said. "I know plenty of people whose fathers don't."

I nodded.

I'd always tried to focus on how things could have been worse. We were able to stay in the house and Mom didn't have to quit a job she loved to find a better paycheck. And then she met Leonard and they married and had Natalie, the greatest gift of all my life, and none of that would have happened if Thaddeus Dean hadn't decided he was destined for a different life as the nation's leading expert on interconnectedness in the digital age with a much younger, childless woman he'd met, no joke: online.

I found myself sharing all of this with Daphne even though I'd pretty much stopped telling people the story of my father. I let those who didn't know better assume Leonard was my biodad, though anyone with eyes should have seen through that. I hadn't even talked about my father that much with Penny, though once, we Google-imaged him—he'd grown a beard and had started wearing wire-rimmed glasses.

"He's kind of handsome," Penny said.

"I guess so."

"Like you. But you're way hotter."

"So when's the last time you saw him?" Daphne asked me.

"When I was about five. At first he used to see me once a month. Then twice a year. Then . . ."

"Does he live far away?"

"Nope."

He'd moved to San Francisco a few years ago to run some technology think tank. Before that, he lived in London and Sydney. I knew all this from checking his online trail now and then. Mom and I never talked about him anymore.

"So . . . he's an expert on how the Internet brings people closer together?"

"Yeah."

"And yet . . . he never even emails you?"

"Not once."

"So he's your why."

"I'm not sure about that."

"I am."

I looked around. The restaurant had nearly emptied out without my noticing. Guys from the kitchen were sweeping floors and putting chairs up on tables, pouring the remains of ketchup bottles one into the other. It was time to go home.

"I wonder what happened to Mason and Christopher?"

"Maybe they went out for a pack of smokes," she said. "And they're never coming back."

They were sitting on the hood of Christopher's car, windows down, radio playing. The night was beautiful. Balmy with a violet sky.

We dropped Daphne off first. She lived in a little box of a house surrounded by a waist-high chain link fence. A postage-stamp-sized front yard littered with plastic toddler toys. A palm tree that listed to the right. She unlocked a metal security gate and then a front door. We waited until she'd closed both behind her before hopping back on the 10. Despite feeling a world away, I was back at my house in twenty minutes.

Mom was at the door when I arrived.

"Who was that?" she asked, watching the taillights of Christopher's Audi round the corner.

"Friends."

"I figured they weren't enemies. I mean, which friends? I don't recognize that car."

"Just some guys I know."

I could tell Mom was trying to set the stage for one of our late-night talks. Leonard's workday started before sunrise, so he went to bed early like Natalie. Mom and I were night owls. Sometimes we hung out in the kitchen talking way past midnight. Usually we'd eat an entire fourth meal.

"Omelet?" she asked.

"Nah, I'm going to bed."

She looked disappointed, but I was tired and missing Penny. It was only ten forty-five. We used to stay together until eleven-thirty on Saturday nights, her curfew.

I lay down on my bed in my clothes. I couldn't help but wonder what Penny had done tonight. And I couldn't help but wonder if she'd wondered about me. Maybe she'd stayed home and watched a movie with Ben. Maybe her dad had grilled steaks in the backyard. It had been that kind of night. Whatever she'd imagined when she thought of me, or if she'd even thought of me, I knew she hadn't pictured me walking nearly five miles to A Second Chance support group for teens. Yup. It was absurd. But Penny believed I didn't think about things. That I didn't reflect. So if she'd stretched out on her bed tonight and wondered about me, I doubted she'd imagined I'd spent the evening talking about my battle with drugs to a roomful of strangers and then talking about my father for so long that a restaurant had emptied. I'd done nothing tonight but think. Reflect. Now that I thought back on the past few hours, I regretted how much I'd talked to Daphne. I'd talked so much about myself that I'd never even asked what her father did at his two jobs. I hadn't asked about her mom. Or her brothers and sisters.

I pulled out my phone. I wanted to text Penny, but I didn't. For one thing, Maggie had deleted her contact information, not that I didn't know it by heart, but Maggie thought if I had to take the time to actually dial in Penny's number, I might stop and realize what I was doing and think better of it.

I texted Daphne. The four of us had exchanged numbers when we'd dropped her off. We'd talked about maybe working out some sort of car pool situation, though I didn't mention I had no car. Or license.

ME: What does UR dad do?

HER: WTF?

ME: What does UR dad do on his night shifts?

HER: Warehouse worker/baker

ME: Mom?

HER: No, it's Daphne

ME: Duh. I mean, what does UR mom do?

HER: Housekeeper

ME: What R UR siblings names?

HER: Maria, Miguel, Claudia, Roberto

ME: Thx. G-night Daphne

HER: G-night boy w/ the unforgettable name

EIGHT

When I met Will at the beginning of freshman year, with his high voice and long hair and short-shorts, I'd never have imagined the senior-year version, the Will to whom girls, grades and great parking spaces came effortlessly.

But back to the shorts. When I say short I mean *really* short. I mean an inch away from sharing your balls with the world short.

We were getting ready for PE. I hadn't noticed Will at the locker next to me, but once I saw those shorts, it was hard to look away.

It wasn't until a few weeks later, after we'd started hanging out, that I said, "Dude. Those shorts. They need to go." We'd just run laps.

He looked down. "These? Really?" And then he took off for one final lap, which we later called "the lap of shame."

I didn't see those shorts again until my birthday months

later. I was surprised he'd brought a wrapped gift to school.
Even a card.

Dear River—to mark the occasion of you turning 15,
here: something that says how much you mean to me
better than words.

I unwrapped it. The shorts.

Over the years we'd found ways to give them back and
forth. I'd leave them in his car or his backpack. He'd sneak
into my room and put them in my drawer. I sent them to
his summer camp in a care package. But no one ever wore
them.

Until he walked into my kitchen that Thursday morning.

"Hurry up, River. I'll drive you to school."

Will had grown since freshman year so the shorts had
reached a whole new level of . . . inappropriate. Mom
stared, openmouthed.

"What is it, Deb?" He spun around. "Is there something
in my teeth?"

"William Parker," she said. "What on earth are you
wearing?"

He slung an arm around her shoulder. "Deb, River needs
cheering up. And these shorts bring joy to the world."

"If it wouldn't make us late," I said, "I'd make you take
a lap of shame."

I dragged him to my room and threw him a pair of my
jeans. We laughed most of the way to school.

My good mood lasted until right before sixth-period study hall, when I practically tripped over the table where Penny's best friend, Vanessa, sat with a box of cash and a pile of printed purple tickets.

"Hey, River—how *are* you?" She asked this like she'd ask *How are you since someone ran over your puppy?* Or *How are you since your face got disfigured?* "Going to the dance? It should be super fun. Penny is going." She held up a single ticket. "The theme is Purple Rain."

I couldn't think of anything to say. My mind was a blizzard of thick, soft snow.

That night at Jonas's party Penny and I took a walk around the block together and I grabbed her hand and told her I was going to kiss her and she said: *What are you waiting for?*

I leaned in close. I put both of my hands on her cheeks. We were standing out on the street, under a tree, in front of a house where the lights had just gone out. She was chewing that blue sugar-free gum she loved.

I can't say that the kiss was perfect. I'd liked her since freshman orientation and I was having a hard time just being in the moment because my brain kept screaming *I'M ABOUT TO KISS PENNY BROCKAWAY.* But the kiss was good enough that afterward she pulled back and bit her upper lip. It was the first time I made note of her habit. She smiled at me. "Let's go someplace and do more of that."

I dropped my jaw in fake shock. *"You little tramp!"* I said. "Do you think I'm that easy?" Then I leaned in again and gave her a short peck, the kind you give someone you've been kissing forever, not the girl you've only kissed once a minute ago. But it already felt like I'd been kissing Penny forever, not in the way that you're bored with doing it, more in the way that it felt like second nature.

We walked holding hands for three more blocks to a park I took Natalie to sometimes.

We sat on a bench away from the lights and we kissed until we both had red rashes around our mouths. I felt drunk. My hair was a mess from the way she ran her hands through it. Penny always did love my hair.

I wondered what it would be like at school the following Monday. Would I know how to talk to her? Would it be awkward? Would she want to sit with me at lunch? But all of a sudden we were a couple. It was easy. I never worried where things stood with us until the afternoon I pedaled her out to the middle of Echo Park Lake.

"I can't go," I said to Vanessa.

"Why not?" She sounded genuinely disappointed.

"I'm busy."

"Too bad." She put the ticket back into the box. "I guess I should let you know that Penny is going with Evan Lockwood."

Snow. Falling hard inside my head.

"Don't tell her I told you, okay? I don't want her to be mad, but . . . I feel like it's only fair if you know."

Before I knew what I was doing, I was opening my wallet and buying two tickets.

"Are these for you and Maggie?" she asked. Vanessa knew Maggie and I were just friends.

"No."

She counted out each dollar and flattened it.

She handed over the tickets. "See you and . . . whoever there."

I was late to study hall, and I slid into my seat next to Luke, who stared at the tickets in my hand like I'd just walked in carrying a rubber chicken or a hamster.

"The dance?"

I shrugged.

I'd avoided school dances like . . . well, school dances. I'd never been to one until I started going out with Penny. She liked getting dressed up, picking out an outfit for me, walking around clinging to my arm, and pulling me close for a slow song. The rest of the time she'd dance with her friends—that was more fun for her and also more humane, because nobody needed to see me dance. It wasn't pretty.

Luke never went and Will had only been to one dance because a girl he didn't like that much caught him off guard and asked him and he didn't have the heart to say no. Maggie went sometimes with other girls, mostly just to spy on people. But now that we were seniors, regular dances seemed especially stupid because the year was going to end with a prom anyway.

"I guess I just thought maybe we should go."

"Are you asking me to the dance?"

"Sort of."

"Dude. Have you completely lost your mind?"

"*Shhhhhhhhhhh.*" Mr. Baumgarten, our study hall proctor, looked up from his pile of papers.

Evan Lockwood played basketball with Luke. Maybe Luke knew that Evan had asked Penny to the dance, or maybe Vanessa had her facts wrong.

Luke took out a sheet of paper and wrote: *Get a grip. Don't go to the dance to stalk Penny.*

Solid advice, but instead of tearing up the tickets I put them away in my wallet.

I didn't do any work. I just tried to erase the image of Penny pressed against Evan Lockwood during some cheesy Bruno Mars song.

For the rest of the afternoon those tickets burned a hole in my wallet. What if I went to Penny's house with those tickets and got down on a knee even, and said something like: *Penny Brockaway, will you do me the honor of going to the Purple Rain dance with me?*

Would Penny fall for a gesture like that? Part of me thought she might, judging from the number of romantic comedies she'd made me sit through. When we'd watch those movies—a bowl of popcorn, my arm around her shoulder, her legs draped across my lap, Nuisance curled up next to us on the couch—I felt like she was trying to teach me about how to be the dreamy boyfriend, the one who always does and says the right thing, and when he doesn't, he makes it up to his girlfriend in just the right way.

Guys in those movies wouldn't sit by and let Evan Lockwood take their girlfriends to the Purple Rain dance without a fight.

"I need a ride," I said over dinner.

"Where to?" Mom asked.

73

"Penny's house."

"I thought you broke up." Leonard said this without making eye contact, like it was no big deal, like you'd say *Nice weather we're having.*

"They did," Natalie chimed in. "But Penny and I can still be friends."

I smiled at her. "At least there's that."

"So are you two patching things up?" I loved Mom. I really did. But sometimes her expressions were just so old person-y.

"I hope so." When nobody said anything I added, "I bought us tickets to the dance."

"Tickets to the dance." That was a habit of Leonard's: repeating something I said when he didn't like what I was saying. Like when I mentioned I wanted to drop precalc because why torture myself when I'd already fulfilled my math requirements. *Dropping precalculus,* he'd said.

"Yes, I thought I'd go over tonight and ask her to be my date to the dance."

"Oh, honey." Mom patted my arm. "Why don't you just give her a call? You don't need to go over there so late at night."

"It's only seven-thirty."

"Yes, but . . ."

"But what?"

"But . . . maybe you should give her some space?"

This was not what the guys in the romantic comedies did, they didn't give space, but I couldn't tell Mom this. She wouldn't understand. Over the last two years Mom had gently tried—many times—to tell me that I focused too much of my attention on Penny, that I should back off a little, not let my relationship be the center of my universe. But I ignored her because she was my mother. What did she know?

"Buddy." This was Leonard's signal that he was speaking with authority, about something beyond the realm of Mom's expertise. I never minded when Leonard played this part, even if I didn't always agree with him. Leonard meant well, and he was often right. I still wish I'd dropped precalc, though.

"Maybe it's better to let her realize what she's missing? You could even ask someone else to the dance. You know what they say about fish in the sea and all that."

"Yeah, they're full of mercury poisoning."

I was starting to feel sort of pathetic, and I didn't want to make it worse by begging them for a ride, so I just excused myself and went to my room.

But those tickets. The image of me on one knee with them fanned in my hand, looking up at a surprised and delighted Penny. It wouldn't leave me alone.

Penny's house was a thirty-minute walk, twenty-five if I hustled. I didn't want to take all those minutes because now it was starting to get late, and I didn't want her to be in pajamas or anything. That wasn't how I imagined it all going down.

I climbed out my window. I'd done this lots of times,

often when I wasn't even headed anyplace but the backyard. Sometimes it was just nice to come and go without
getting noticed.

Leonard's truck was in the garage and the keys hung on
the hook. He'd taken me driving a few times. I was pretty
sure I could make the trip to Penny's without causing a
multivehicle pileup, but the last thing I needed was to do
something illegal. I didn't want to give Mom and Leonard
any more cause to worry about my judgment.

Natalie had gotten a new bike for her birthday a few
months back. She was in between frame sizes so Leonard
bought her the next size up to grow into. Her feet barely
touched the ground when she sat on the seat and this made
her spooked about riding it, so she hadn't yet.

I took it on its inaugural ride, pedaling standing up the
whole way because I couldn't sit without knocking my
knees into my chin. My overall appearance on this bike
wasn't helped by the fact that it was hot pink. I looked absurd. But it was dark. And I was on a mission.

As I approached Penny's block I hopped off the bike
and stashed it in the tall hedges of a neighbor's front yard.
I caught my breath. Wiped my palms on my jeans and
slowed to a casual walk.

I found Juana in the driveway, dragging the black garbage bins out to the street.

"*Hola*, Juana."

I'd startled her. She jumped and put her hand to her
chest, but then didn't seem all that relieved to discover it
was me.

"Hi, River."

"Here, let me help you." I walked back up the driveway with her and grabbed a recycling bin. She grabbed the other and we dragged them down to the street together.

"Why are you here, River?" she asked.

"To see Penny."

"I'm not so sure that's a good idea."

"But I have tickets," I said. "For the dance."

"Yes," she said. "Penelope has a new dress. It's purple."

"Does she have a date?"

"River, I can't—"

"Never mind."

I knew. Vanessa was telling the truth.

Maybe Penny and Evan Lockwood had been secretly planning to go to that dance together long before the tickets went on sale. Maybe Penny had been thinking about Evan Lockwood when she said, "Riv, I can't do this anymore."

I stood looking up at Penny's huge house. Every light seemed to be on. This house had been my second home, and now here I stood, out with the garbage bins.

"Maybe don't tell her I came by. Is that okay, Juana?"

"Yes. It's okay, River. I won't say a word."

I went and retrieved Natalie's bike from the hedges and I pedaled sitting down, knees splayed and aching, all the way home.

NiNE

I needed more than my spotty memories of those junior high Say No to Drugs assemblies, so I turned to the Internet for material to use in my Saturday-night meeting.

I searched: *teenage + marijuana + addiction*.

Mostly I uncovered facts I knew—that marijuana is bad for brain development, it's stronger than it used to be and it can act as a gateway drug. Some experts argue it's not possible to have an addiction to marijuana, while others document addiction in a small percentage of users.

I eventually stumbled upon the blog of an anonymous teenage boy living in an undisclosed Midwestern city who took to the Internet to chronicle his struggle with marijuana addiction in the hope of helping others in his situation, or in my case, others who might be trying to pretend to be in his situation.

Bam: interconnectedness in the digital age!

This kid started getting high the summer after eighth grade and what began as a weekend activity morphed into an everyday activity until he got busted. He said he'd stop but he didn't, until he got busted again and said he'd stop for real. But then his days felt so long and dull, and he couldn't find anything that quieted his constant agitation, so he kept smoking, and when he finally got busted the third time his parents sent him into rehab for a thirty-day detox and he came out and started a blog: *itainteasybeinoffgreen*.

For Saturday's meeting I homed in on this entry from a few weeks back.

I went to a party last night and it was kind of okay because the music wasn't awful. Some music makes me want to get high so bad because it's music I used to listen to when I'd get baked and I have this physical need to hold a joint in my hand. I can almost taste it. And some music makes me want to get high because it makes me depressed, like that Emo crap. But last night at this party the music was okay because it was neither of those things and I was in a good mood because I was with my friends and we were hanging out and laughing and then some douche asks if anyone wants to get high. I said no. He said why not? You scared? And I said no, it's just that I'm addicted to marijuana. And he laughed in my face. It totally ruined my night. I had to leave. I can't even be anywhere near weed. I'm too weak.

Because . . . it ain't easy bein off green.

Peace out.

★   ★   ★

Okay. So maybe he wasn't Shakespeare but he did give me someone to inhabit. Someone to plagiarize.

Christopher skipped the meeting. It hadn't occurred to me to worry about someone with a love for euphoria-inducing drugs blowing off group therapy on a Saturday night, but Everett opened the circle by saying, "I want to assuage any concerns you might have about Christopher. He isn't here tonight because he had a family event to attend—his cousin's Bat Mitzvah. He'll rejoin us next week."

I'd never seen Molly at a Bat Mitzvah, so Christopher would probably be just fine.

I was bummed he wasn't there because I'd hoped for a repeat of the week before. That was fun. And I'd been counting on not having to walk the five miles home.

After our call and response—Here, This, Now—Everett said, "Tonight I want you to tell us something good. Tell us something true."

Daphne took a long time getting started. She seemed less animated than usual. Maybe she was missing Christopher. "So . . ." She stopped. "So . . ." More silence. "Something true . . ." She looked carefully at her fingernails. She'd repainted them from light pink to dark blue. "Something true is that I'm tired." More silence. "I'm so tired."

"Can you—"

"Yes, I can say more, Everett," she snapped. "Obviously I know by now that just saying *I'm tired* isn't going to cut it in here. So yeah, I'm tired because I get up every morning at six to make breakfast for me and everybody and then I take the little one to the neighbor's house, and then I get the middle two to school. My sister Maria, she's big enough to take care of herself but she still expects me to make her breakfast and pack her lunch, because that's what I do. And sometimes, when I'm taking Roberto over to this lady's house? Where he stays all day with a couple other kids? Sometimes I feel like maybe I should just quit school and watch him, because what's the point? Is this why my parents work so hard? Why my dad works night shifts? Why my mom cleans another family's house and takes care of other people's kids? So that they can pay for someone else to watch their *own* kid? Sometimes . . . it all just seems pointless." She leaned forward, arms on knees, and stared at the floor.

"And something good . . ." Daphne lifted her head and stared right at me. I felt my body go insta-hot, like all the air had just left the room. I looked away, because I didn't want her to see me react, but then when I snuck a look at her I realized she wasn't looking at me at all, she was focusing on a spot on the wall just above my head.

"Something good . . ." She brought her gaze back to the circle. "Something good is Roberto. The little one? He calls me *Mamá* sometimes. He's so beautiful, that boy. He's just got this big, perfect heart, you know? And this week, we were walking to the neighbor's house, and I was holding his little hand, and he says to me, *Te amo, Mamá,* and I tell him I love him too, and then he says *You're pretty,* and I say *You love me because I'm pretty?* And he says *No, I love you because you're brave and strong, like a ninja."* Daphne smiled and put both hands to her chest. "He kills me."

When the circle came around to me I started with something good. I thought about my crappy week. About Penny's new purple dress and my incomplete precalc homework, about how I'd Googled my father even though I'd sworn to myself I wouldn't, and how he'd trimmed his beard back to the look of someone too busy to shave and switched his glasses from round wire to square wire frames.

"My good is my sister Natalie." I looked at Daphne. "She doesn't think I'm a ninja or anything, in fact I'm pretty sure she's totally aware of my shortcomings, but still, she worships me. All she wants is for us to share a last name. To be even closer than we already are. And I . . . I want to be the person she believes me to be."

I felt that frog throat thing happening so I took a few long swallows. I'd used Natalie as my good, but she was also my true. What I'd said about her was as true as anything I know.

"And something true . . . ," I said. Daphne's eyes were dark and shining and not focused on any spot above my head, but right on me. No hand motions needed. There was an understanding—something about me she connected to something inside herself. "Something true . . ."

This would have been the perfect moment to admit I wasn't addicted to pot. That I came here each week because I was trying to figure out who I was and who I wanted to be.

I cleared my throat. "Something true is that I went to a party last night and it was kind of okay because the music wasn't awful . . ."

Mason's mother stood waiting outside on the sidewalk. How someone like him could have come from someone like her was a mystery of science. Everything about her was tiny, her face, her ears, her feet. She couldn't have stood more than five feet tall.

He embraced her and she disappeared. Then he took her tiny hand and led her over to Daphne and me.

"These are my friends. Beautiful, amazing Daphne, and River, who is sweet but full of shit." He shot me a semi-apologetic look. "Sorry. Bad Mason." He slapped his own wrist. "And this . . . is my mommy." He stood back, displaying her proudly. "You guys don't mind sacrificing your anonymity to meet the greatest woman God ever created, do you?"

Daphne and I shook our heads.

"Well then, thank you for being a friend to my son," she said. "For listening and being here each week. For doing what you do to help him become his best self. Now let's go, honey." She turned to Mason. "We don't want to be late."

He linked his arm through hers. "Got a movie to catch," he called over his shoulder as they walked down the street toward her car. "Later, people."

When Natalie was a baby, Mom and I had a standing Saturday-night movie date. We'd alternate the kinds of movies I liked—action or science fiction—with the kinds she liked—mostly stories of women on a journey of rediscovery after being disappointed by men. We'd share popcorn and a Milk Duds. We hadn't been to a movie together in years.

"I didn't see that coming," I said to Daphne after they disappeared. Without Christopher and his cigarettes, we had no excuse for loitering.

"Whaddya mean?" she asked.

"You know." I made motions with my hands that indicated Mason's large size and then his mother's diminutiveness.

"Oh." She laughed. "She's his foster mom. She didn't, like, birth him or anything."

"That explains it."

"Yeah, I guess you've missed a lot. See, Mason spent most of his childhood moving around, home to home, bad to worse, until he wound up in Culver City with this mom. She's the first person to love him, you know, like, no matter what. He's been with her since he was thirteen. And she's given him everything. Support. Stability. She even sends him to a fancy school. And yet . . . sometimes he still barfs into jars and hides them under his bed. Go figure."

I didn't know much about bulimia, but I'd always assumed only girls had it. Blond, skinny, insecure girls, not big brutes like Mason. It was easy to forgive him being hard on me because he'd been through so much, and also because he was right. I was full of shit.

"Do you wanna do something?" Daphne asked.

"Like what?"

"I don't know. I just don't feel like going home yet."

"And you want to do something with *me*?"

"Jeez, River. I just wanted to know if you wanna, like, do something or eat something or just kill some time. I'm not trying to date you or anything."

"I didn't mean it like that." Why was I always embarrassing myself in front of Daphne? "I meant, without Christopher around I just wasn't sure you'd want to hang out."

"Christopher? I don't like Christopher. Not like that anyway."

"You sure?"

"Why do you care so much?"

"I don't."

"Christopher isn't for me. He's a rich kid with a club drug habit. Not my type."

"Duly noted."

"So let's go somewhere. You got your car?"

"Uh . . . I don't have one."

"You don't have a car? What kind of Westside boy are you, anyway?"

"The kind without a car. Or a license."

"You don't have a license?"

"Nope. I don't drive."

It occurred to me that the only reason Daphne had asked me to do something was probably because she wanted a ride home. I braced myself for a blowoff.

She shrugged. "So I guess we're gonna have to walk somewhere."

"*That* I know how to do."

We walked south toward Venice Boulevard, where I'd remembered seeing a taco stand that drew a crowd. The picnic benches outside were filled, and when she spied two free seats she went to secure them. I got on line and brushed off her attempt to give me money.

She put her hand on her hip and arched her eyebrows at me. "I told you this isn't a date."

"I know. Chill out. I'm just buying you a taco."

"No, you're buying me two tacos."

We sat for a while after we were done eating, sipping our Jarritos sodas—strawberry for her, mango for me. I could feel the cavities blooming.

"So how do you get around, River? You already said you don't take the bus because"—and here she put on a funny accent I knew was supposed to sound like a white person, but came off like an über-nerd—*"Nobody takes the bus in LA."*

"Promise you won't judge me?"

"I can't promise that."

"My girlfriend drove me everywhere. We were together before we turned sixteen and she got her license first, so I never needed to get mine. And I have friends who drive too, so . . ."

"That's pathetic."

I'd been told this before. Lots of times. But it was the first time I saw the truth in it.

"Do you have a license?"

"Of course I do. I just don't have a car." She reached over and took my mango soda and took a sip of it without asking first. I looked at the bottle top for a trace of her pink lip gloss, but she didn't leave any behind. "You know what I'm gonna do for you, River?"

"Nope."

"I'm gonna teach you how to ride the bus."

"Thanks, but—"

"No need to thank me. I like a charity case now and then. You'll be like my community service project. I can put it on my college applications. I'll be all: *Volunteered time to help poor Westside white boy understand how to navigate the Los Angeles public transportation system.*"

"Ha."

"Ha."

Her arm rested on the table and I took a close look at her wrist tattoo. It was beautiful. I wanted to ask her about it but I didn't.

"So you're going to college next year?"

"Why wouldn't I be?"

"I didn't mean it like that. I—"

"At some point, yeah, I'm going to go to college. But not next year. I don't know what my parents would do without me. And I don't have the money. And I haven't figured out how to steal it."

"Daphne—"

"Kidding. What about you, River? You going to college next year?"

"My applications are in. I'll hear in a few weeks. And I have the money. But I don't want it. The money, I mean."

"Say what?"

"It's from my father. My mom and Leonard can't afford it, but he can. That was the deal. He'll pay for college. And I'll go on about my life and occasionally stalk him on the Internet."

"You have to take his money, River. Not taking his money would be more stupid than trying to steal it."

"I know, it's just—"

"It's just that you want to prove you don't need him."

"I guess so."

"Here's the thing. He owes you. Big-time. He owes you more than a college education."

"Should I ask him to buy me a pony?"

"At least then you wouldn't have to ride the bus."

Music played softly in the background, and multicolored Christmas lights hung over the picnic tables like a circus of stars. A celebration in the cosmos. She smiled at me, and for the first time since that day in the middle of Echo Park Lake, I felt happy enough to be sitting right here, not wondering what Penny was doing, where she was doing it and with whom.

I wanted to tell Daphne that she needed to go to college too. That she was too smart to stay home playing babysitter to her siblings. That there had to be a way. But I didn't know how to say what I wanted to. For the first time, I saw how lucky I was.

"Do you want another taco?"

"No."

"Another soda?" I wasn't ready for the night to be over.

"No."

She reached behind her for her purse. "Come on. Let's hit the bus stop. Your lesson starts now."

TEN

I sat with Maggie and Will in the gym watching Luke's basketball game, sizing up Evan Lockwood.

"He does have magnificent thighs," Maggie sighed. "But he doesn't have nearly as much going for him overall as you do, River. For one thing, he's not as cute."

"River is cute?" Will cocked his head at me.

"Duh. Look at him. Cute in that sensitive, vulnerable, pretty boy sort of way."

"I'd trade any one of those for magnificent thighs," I said.

"Jesus," Will said. "Stop saying *magnificent thighs*."

Maggie gave him a shove. "Oh my god! That should be your band name! Will Parker and the Magnificent Thighs. I'm calling the booker at Largo!"

If you'd been watching me on those bleachers, smiling and laughing, you'd never have known that on the inside I was like those antismoking photos they show you in health class: charred and sickly. How could Penny consider going anywhere with Evan Lockwood? With anyone but me?

"I'm sorry she dumped you, River," Maggie said. "But I'd be lying if I said that sorry is the only thing I felt."

"I know you guys didn't like her."

"It's not that we didn't like her, it's that we didn't like you with her."

"Yeah," Will added. "You were kind of a pussy."

"Hey! I was just a good boyfriend."

"No, you were pretty much a major pussy."

Maggie smacked Will on the back of the head. "That word is demeaning and stupid. And you're better than that." She turned to me. "But, River, you did do whatever Penny told you to. And the truth, which Will can't properly express because he's a Neanderthal, is that we missed you."

Just then, Evan Lockwood scored a three-point shot. The gym went berserk.

"Wow. I really bollixed everything up, didn't I?"

"Sorta," Will said.

"It's too bad there isn't some girl you could ask to the dance. And I'm not suggesting me, because I'm obviously a pity date and that just looks sad and desperate. How about . . ." Maggie scanned the crowd and then pointed across the gym. "Her?"

"Rachel Pomeroy? Uh . . . no thank you."

"Why?"

"She's mean. And scary."

"So?"

"Well, mean and scary aren't qualities I look for in a mate."

"Nobody said anything about mating. We said you need a date for the dance so that Penny can see you're moving on. It's time to remake your image. You need somebody a little intimidating. Someone who might knock Penny's sense of superiority down a notch."

That was when Daphne came to me. In Day-Glo. She was perfect. Intimidating and beautiful with the added bonus of being unknown.

But how to explain Daphne to my friends? How could I know someone from Boyle Heights when I didn't even drive? How had I struck up a friendship with a Mexican girl who was raising her siblings because her parents worked three jobs around the clock?

A friendship with Daphne challenged every presumption of the life I'd been leading for seventeen years. Everyone I knew was a different variation on the same Westside theme. We all went to schools with nice gyms and impressive college matriculation records. Some of us were richer (Penny), some were poorer (me), some were whiter (Maggie could trace her family back to the *Mayflower*) and some less so (Luke's mother was a doctor from Mexico City).

Nobody I knew was like Daphne . . . Crap. I didn't even know her last name.

This was going to be a tough one.

Luke's team lost the game and we went to our usual diner for a consolation sundae. It felt good to be a quadrangle again.

"So I met this girl . . . online," I said.

"You what?"

"I met this girl."

"Online."

"Yes."

Maggie looked at Will and then at Luke. They both stared back blankly, like: *Don't ask us, we're just guys, we don't understand anything.* "River, I had no idea things had gotten that desperate," she said.

"I wasn't, like, online dating or whatever." My mind spun. How was I going to explain this?

"So . . . how *did* you meet a girl?" Luke asked.

"Well, I didn't *meet a girl.* I mean . . . I don't *like* her. We're just friends."

"Okay. So how did you meet this girl you don't like on-line?" Will asked.

"On Instagram."

"Wait. Hold on." Maggie pushed up her sleeves. "You have an Instagram account?"

"Yes."

"But you hate Instagram. In fact, you hate all social media."

"I know. But I suddenly have more time on my hands without Penny and I decided to check out Instagram."

Maggie whipped out her phone. "What's your user name?"

"I'm not going to tell you that."

"River," she said, putting down her phone. "Let me explain how Instagram works. You tell your friends what your user name is so that they can follow you so that you can get more followers so that you aren't alone out there in the wilds of the Internet."

"Yeah . . . but . . ." I was treading water. "This is, like, a new thing for me. Something separate from my normal life. I'm trying to take more risks. To be less . . . predictable."

"So what's your deal? Like, do you have a thing?"

"Huh?"

"I mean, do you have some sort of Instagram identity? Something that sets you apart? Are you posting pictures of anything in particular or just your dull, boring life as a heartbroken loser? Because that's, you know, pretty predictable."

For some reason Daphne's tattoo popped into my mind, the roses on the vine that wound around her wrist.

"Tattoos."

"Tattoos?"

"Yeah. I post pictures of tattoos."

"River." Now Maggie pulled down the sleeves she'd just pushed up. "Do I need to state the obvious? That you don't have a tattoo?"

"I know I don't have a tattoo, but I like them. I think they're . . . beautiful. And I take pictures of other people's tattoos and post them on Instagram."

Maggie looked at Will and Luke. They shrugged.

"I can't escape the feeling," she said, glancing at the ceiling since the guys weren't offering any help, "that I've stepped into an alternate universe. Someplace where River

Dean takes artsy pictures of strangers' tattoos and posts them online."

"Dude," Luke said. "That's kinda awesome."

"Thanks."

"So you met this girl . . ." Maggie gave me the *go on* motion.

"Yeah, I met this girl. And she likes my pictures. And she has a tattoo of roses on a vine that wind around her wrist."

"Sexy," Will said.

I nodded noncommittally. "She's cool. Her name's Daphne. I think maybe I should invite her to the dance, you know, as a friend."

"Where does she go to school?" Luke asked.

"I don't know."

Maggie frowned. "Are you sure she's not some forty-three-year-old perv masquerading as a high school girl with a cool tattoo?"

"Nah, I've hung out with her."

"When?"

"Just a couple of times. Listen, should I ask her or would it be awkward?"

"We'll go as a group. That'll kill the awkward."

Suddenly Will perked up. "What do you mean by *we*?"

"I mean you and me and River and tattoo girl will go to the dance together. And Luke too if he wants to."

Luke put his hands up. "I don't want to."

"Neither do I," said Will.

"That's too bad." Maggie threw an arm around Will. "Because we're going. And you're driving."

That night I texted Daphne.

ME: Hey

HER: Hey

ME: What R U doing?

HER: Texting U

ME: Duh

HER: So?

ME: So do U wanna go to a dance w/me Fri?

HER:

ME: Well do U?

HER:

ME: Hello?

HER: Hi

ME: Is that a no?

HER: R U really asking me to a dance in a text?

She answered before I even heard her phone ring.

"This is Daphne."

"Hi, Daphne. It's River."

"River who? I know several Rivers."

"River Dean."

"Oh, that River. Hi, River Dean."

"Hi, Daphne . . ."

"Vargas."

"Hi, Daphne Vargas. This is River Dean calling. I was wondering if by any chance you'd want to come with me to a dance at my school this Friday night."

A long pause. Long enough for nerves I didn't even know I had to kick in.

"I just thought . . . I don't know. Maybe it would be sort of fun. In a stupid way. It doesn't have to be a real date or anything."

"Is that code for you want me to go with you to make your ex-girlfriend jealous?"

"No . . ."

"That's okay. I don't mind."

"You don't?"

"Nah. I like the challenge."

"Cool. Is that a yes?"

The line went quiet.

"If it helps you make up your mind, the theme is Purple Rain."

"I don't understand what that means."

"I don't really either."

Another pause. "I'm not sure this is such a good idea, River."

"Why?"

"Well . . . I take what happens at our meetings seriously. And you know, there are rules about this sort of stuff. Did you ever read that yellow pamphlet?"

"Yeah . . . but . . . it's not a date. Why is it any different than going for a French dip? Or Jarritos and tacos?"

She was silent. Then, "I guess it's not."

"So that's a yes?"

"It's a sure. Why not."

"Cool. I'll pick you up."

"You don't drive, remember? You like to walk."

"My friend Will drives. And . . . there's more."

"What more could there be than a Purple Rain theme?"

"Well, my friends don't know about A Second Chance. That's a secret. So I told them we met online."

"Ew."

"No, like on Instagram."

"I'm not on Instagram."

"I'm not either. But I told them I have an Instagram account where I post pictures of other people's tattoos and you liked my pictures and we became friends."

"Weird."

"I know. It's all I could come up with on the spot. I just . . . didn't want them to know."

"Do they know you have a marijuana addiction?"

"Do your friends know you shoplift?"

A long silence.

"No. Nobody knows but my parents. The police were kind enough to inform them. They were so proud."

I thought about how difficult that moment must have been for her. Daphne—the girl who holds it all together.

"But they must be proud of you now? How hard you work for everything and how hard you're working on yourself?"

"Yeah, I guess they are."

Maybe I should have just asked Rachel Pomeroy. It didn't seem fair to enlist Daphne in my stupid plot to make Penny jealous—she had more important battles to fight.

"Look, Daphne. Maybe you have a point. Maybe this isn't such a great idea."

"Are you *un*inviting me to the dance?"

"No, I just don't want to put you on the spot or make you uncomfortable or—"

"River. Do you know when the last time I went to a school dance was? Or really, the last time I did anything just for fun?"

"No."

"I don't either. So I think I'd like to go."

"You're sure? Because—"

"I'm sure."

"Great." I exhaled. I hadn't even noticed I'd been holding my breath. "Oh, and one more thing you need to know."

"What?"

"I'm a terrible dancer."

ELEVEN

"So who's the lucky girl?" Mom asked.

"There is no lucky girl. I'm just going with friends."

"Well." She reached over and brushed my hair out of my eyes: her not-so-subtle way of letting me know I should have gotten a haircut before the dance. "I'm just glad you're going and not moping around the house."

"Have I been moping?" I thought I'd gotten the pity party under control.

She straightened my tie. "I know you're hurt, River. But it's a good time for a reset. Time to dig back into your own life. It's the last months of your senior year. You've worked hard. You shouldn't have a care in the world."

I thought about Daphne and all her problems. About Christopher, Mason and the others. Mom was right. I should have been carefree, but I couldn't help it; I still felt like I was alone in a boat in the middle of a lake.

Natalie came bounding into the room. "Your tie is too fat. You should wear the other one."

I only had two and that Natalie knew this shouldn't have come as a surprise, though I never in a million years could have told you how many headbands or barrettes or pairs of tights she had.

"Come on." She took me by the hand and led me back to my room. She opened my closet and pushed my clothes out of the way so that she could reach the hook in the back where my other tie hung.

"Just how often do you go snooping in my closet?"

"Pretty often," she said.

I removed the red tie with the dolphins on it. She took the blue-and-black-striped one and put it around my neck and then tied it in a regular knot like she was tying her shoelace.

"There." She stepped back. "You look different. Better. You look like a River Marks, not a River Dean."

I pulled her to me and kissed the top of her head. "Thanks, Nat. I don't know what I'd do without you."

Will honked and I said my good-byes. I was his first stop, so I grabbed the front seat.

"Nice tie," he said. I was in the process of undoing Natalie's knot. Will was wearing an open shirt and a blazer with black jeans.

I reached over and changed the radio station. Will liked what I can only describe as girl music, mushy ballads and sugary pop.

"So before we get Maggie," he said. "You wanna tell me what the real story is with this girl?"

"There is no real story."

"So you're totally not into her?"

"Nope."

"So, like, if there was a massive chemical attack and everyone in all of greater Los Angeles perished, but somehow the two of you survived, you'd start walking toward Bakersfield in search of another living female because you just aren't into her at all?"

"In that scenario, I suppose I could be into her."

"Ha. Got you! You like this girl."

"No. I still love Penny."

Will sighed. "But Penny died in the massive chemical attack," he said glumly.

Maggie was waiting outside in her driveway in a long red dress with her hair tied on top of her head in a style that looked both like she'd spent hours on it and like she'd done it in two seconds without a mirror. She wasn't big into makeup, but tonight she had on enough that she seemed five years older. A college woman come back to humor some high school boys by accompanying them to a silly dance.

"Whoa," Will said as we pulled to a stop.

"Yeah. She looks awesome."

She wobbled over to the car, trying to manage her high heels. I unrolled my window.

"I look amazing." She twirled in a circle. "Don't I?"

She started to open the back door and Will shoved me hard.

"Dude. Give her the front seat. What's wrong with you?"

Will never made me give Maggie the front seat, but she

was technically his date, so I jumped out and held the door for her.

She climbed in. "I could get used to this."

Will looked at me in the rearview mirror. "So are you going to tell me where this Internet friend of yours lives?"

I'd been avoiding this moment. Daphne lived not only east of Fairfax, but so far east, it might as well have been another country.

"Boyle Heights."

"Boyle Heights." Maggie thought it over. "Okay. So we should take the 10."

Will shifted out of park. "Let's do it."

Just as I was about to unlatch the front fence, Daphne stepped out of her house and closed both doors behind her. There was only one streetlamp and it cast a weak yellow glow in her yard, just enough for me to see the electric purple of her dress and the way it fit her. Perfectly.

"Purple Rain?" she said as if she owed me an explanation, probably because I just stood there dumbstruck.

"Right. Yeah. Cool."

"So you decided to abandon the theme and go, like, young corporate executive?"

"What? You don't like my tie?"

She took it in her hand and looked at me. "I hate it."

I slipped it off as I led her to the car. I introduced Will and Maggie, who grinned at her stupidly, unable to hide their elation that she was anyone but Penny.

As we merged onto the freeway, Maggie turned down the radio. "So did anyone do any research on tonight's theme?"

"Actually, yeah," Daphne said. "I did."

"Really?" I stared at her.

"'Purple Rain.' It's a Prince song. Also a wacko movie. He's a musical genius, or so people say. I listened to some of his stuff. It's pretty damn good."

Maggie smiled. "I checked him out too. He's tiny!"

"Yeah," Daphne said. "I could, like, wear him in a baby carrier. He's even skinnier than River."

"Leave me out of this."

Daphne grabbed my bicep. "You've got some skinny-ass arms, River."

Maggie laughed. "You should see him in shorts."

Again, the Eastside proved much closer than it was on my mental map of LA. We pulled into the lot and I could see a crowd gathered outside the gym, boys in suits and sports coats, girls in dresses, flowers pinned to shoulders and strapped to wrists (why hadn't I thought of flowers?), and somewhere in that crowd Penny probably stood, maybe with Evan's arm around her waist or his hand clasping hers.

Will put the car in park and Maggie turned to face us.

"Daphne," she said. "You should know there's gonna be this girl here tonight. And River is under the misconception that the sun shines and the moon glows out of her ass. Sorry for being crude."

"No apology necessary."

"Thanks. Anyway, she is not made of unicorns and rainbows and all things pretty and sparkly and perfect. She's just a girl. Kind of average. Not super nice, not super mean. And what we need to do, the three of us, is to take River in there and show him a great time and prove that life goes on when your girlfriend stops loving you, if she ever loved you in the first place, because to me it seemed more like she just loved having a boyfriend she could totally control."

"Ouch," I said.

"Cry me a river, River." Maggie never tired of this joke.

We got out and Maggie took Will's arm and glanced back over her shoulder and glared at me, so I offered Daphne mine and she took hold of my elbow with the hand with the wrist tattoo, and I took a deep breath and we walked from the parking lot up toward the gym doors and the purple light glowing from inside.

I scanned the crowd while trying hard to look like I wasn't scanning the crowd.

"So where is she?" Daphne asked.

"Where's who?"

"Don't play dumb, River. I know you're looking for her. Just point her out when you see her."

And right then, like Daphne had cued her up for me, I saw Penny: head tossed back, laughing. She was wearing her hair in my favorite style—down—and a dark purple dress, almost black. She had on lipstick. Bright red. Like she was playing dress-up.

"There," I said without pointing. Penny stood on the

dance floor, not dancing, surrounded by a group of girls that hovered close to a group of boys including Evan Lockwood. Also not dancing.

"Where?"

How could she not see Penny? It was as if a spotlight shone directly on her from someplace high above.

I turned my back to the dance floor. "The one in the purple dress."

"Well, that helps a lot."

"The one with the reddish hair and the freckles and the red lipstick."

Daphne peered over my shoulder. "Oh. Her."

She took my hand and led me to the dance floor a few feet away, right in the thick of the crowd. I felt totally vulnerable. A zebra in the Serengeti.

"Let's dance," she said.

"But I told you . . ."

"I know, you said you're a terrible dancer. I'll be the judge of that."

The song was something from one of Will's radio stations. Fast and tinny with a guy who sounded like a girl on lead vocals. Daphne started moving and I stood and watched. She gave me a *come on* motion and so I started swaying back and forth a little.

She stepped closer and took both of my hands. "Okay. This is way worse than you said."

"I believe I used the word *terrible*."

"There has to be a stronger word than *terrible* to describe whatever it is you're doing."

She placed my hands on her waist and put her arms around my neck. The song was fast, but she moved me along with her slowly. Penny used to wear a light, flowery perfume I loved, but Daphne smelled like a tropical forest, fruity and earthy and amazing. Her dress felt soft and slippery.

I looked at Daphne but also concentrated on my peripheral vision, where I could see we were being watched. She pulled me closer.

"Much better," she said. "Look at you. You're dancing."

The song morphed into another fast song with androgynous vocals. The dance floor filled, and during the chorus everyone jumped up and down and sang along while Daphne and I still moved slowly, only a few inches separating us. Penny and her circles of girls and boys all danced together now and I wanted to believe she noticed us, but I didn't want to give her the satisfaction of knowing I cared, so I didn't look over to make sure. Instead, I shut off my peripheral vision and focused all of my five senses on Daphne.

Sight: she looked stunning.

Touch: the thin material of her dress meant I could feel her body heat warming up my palms.

Sound: the music annoyed me less than I thought it would.

Smell: tropical forest.

Taste: N/A. I had no idea how she tasted, though if I had to guess, it would be something like cinnamon, but sweeter.

The song ended and she took a step back.

"Okay. We can go now."

"What?"

"Our work here is done."

"But—I want you to have a good time. You said you hadn't done anything fun in forever."

"I'm having fun. But trust me, we should leave now."

Another song was starting. A slow one. I looked around the gym. Penny was definitely watching us. I kept scanning the dance floor until my eyes landed on Will and Maggie, dancing almost as close as Daphne and I had been, though Will was leading Maggie, not the other way around. He dipped her and she laughed and grabbed hold of her bun, keeping it in place.

Daphne pulled me over to them.

"Um, I guess we should go," I said.

Will stopped, midmove, with Maggie still in his arms. "You're not going to get any argument from me."

Maggie looked at Daphne. "It's time to go?"

"Yes."

"Then it's time to go."

I put my arm around Daphne's shoulder. She slipped her arm around my waist. We started heading toward the exit. I didn't look back. I knew who was watching.

TWELVE

The next night I took the bus to A Second Chance. I did the reverse of the route Daphne had taught me and arrived at the meeting twenty minutes early, puffed up with a sense of accomplishment.

I hung around on the sidewalk waiting for Daphne to show until Everett stuck his head out the door and said we were getting started.

"Don't you want to come in, River?"

I didn't. I wanted to tell her about the bus. She'd smile at me and say I'd done well. Her community service project.

I watched the door. Halfway through Mason's story about eating a roll of cookie dough and then feeling too depressed about it to leave the house, Daphne walked in. Rather than taking the empty seat next to me, she crossed the circle and squeezed in next to Christopher.

Maybe before the day Penny broke my heart I wouldn't have interpreted a move like that as some sort of statement, but now I was hyperattuned to the small actions of others, and as I sat there next to that empty seat I thought: *Daphne is mad at me.*

I went back over the night before.

After the dance we went to a diner in Hollywood Maggie knew about where Daphne explained our abrupt departure. "Now she's going to spend the rest of the night wondering why we left so early. Like, we had someplace better to be. A party, maybe. Or you just couldn't wait one more minute before trying to get me out of this dress."

"That dress does beg to be taken off," Maggie said.

"Let's have a look." Will motioned for her to stand up.

"You didn't notice her dress?" Maggie asked. "How on earth could you not have noticed her dress?"

Will shut her down: "I was too busy looking at *your* dress."

Daphne did a walk up and down the aisle of the diner like she was on a fashion runway. Maggie whistled and Will and I applauded. People's heads turned: it was simply not possible to look away from Daphne as she sauntered past tables and turned on her platform heels, and I said to myself, *Yep, this girl went to the Purple Rain dance with me. Me! Take that, world!*

Will spilled ketchup on his nice white shirt. Maggie tried to wipe it clean with a napkin dipped in seltzer. I sat next to Daphne, with my arm draped on the booth behind her, and at one point I almost moved it onto her shoulders because I forgot for a second that she was just a friend.

Then I wondered what it was that made this night feel like a double date: was it me and Daphne or was it Will and Maggie?

Will asked Daphne questions about my tattoo photographs and she told him they were works of art and that I should show them in a gallery, which I thought was maybe taking it a little too far. And I held her arm out—her skin was so soft—and turned it to the right and to the left, letting Will and Maggie admire her wrist tattoo.

They asked about her school and her family and she lit up when she talked about her little brother. The burgers weren't overcooked. The fries were extra crispy. Will and I split the bill. There was some of the milk shake left over and we took it to go and Daphne and I shared it in the backseat on our drive to Boyle Heights. I walked Daphne to her door and I thanked her for at least the fifth time for agreeing to go to the dance and I hugged her, breathing in one last scent of the tropical forest.

The night was pretty damn close to perfect.

So why did she sit near Christopher?

After we dropped Daphne off, Will and Maggie told me I was crazy for not dating her, but I continued to insist we were just friends, and when they asked why, I said: "One: she's probably out of my league. Two: I still love Penny. And three: I'm not ready to date anyone."

"One: she's not *probably* out of your league, she's *totally* out of your league," Maggie said. "And three: it's a good thing you don't want to date anyone, because you need to learn how to be alone. But that brings us to two: why you still love Penny. Seriously, River. Why do you still love Penny? Give me one good reason."

I thought about this as I sat alone in the backseat of Will's car, unable to reach the radio, where the kind of sad song played that made you want to walk through rain with tears streaming down your face. Since Penny broke up with me, I'd relived what it felt like to kiss and touch her, to run my hands through her hair, to make her laugh or smile. I was happy when I made Penny happy, and I'd never questioned whether or not that was a good thing. I'd never questioned us, or her, and maybe this was what Penny meant when she said I didn't think about things, but why would I think about what was wrong when everything felt right to me? And now I worried that I could never love someone else in the same way, and then wondered if I even wanted to love someone else in the same way.

"She was my first love," I said.

"I know, dude," Will said. "But at some point it'll be time for your second love. And it'll be better."

I thought about how Penny had watched us tonight and how maybe she'd gone home and turned away from Evan as he tried to kiss her. And maybe she went into her closet to retrieve a box she'd put high on a shelf, full of all the things that reminded her of me—the necklace with the heart on a string, the portrait I'd paid a hippie in Venice Beach to draw of her, the ticket stubs from Imagine Dragons, a band I didn't love but got tickets to because Penny did. Maybe through the experience of holding each object, our life together started to come back to her, her regret like a visitor in the room whispering: *It's not too late.*

Or . . . no such box existed because she'd thrown everything that reminded her of me into one of the black bins Juana dragged to the street, and at that moment she was in the backseat of Evan Lockwood's car tangled up in his magnificent thighs.

Penny and Evan. It made me slightly less sick than it had the day before. I didn't want to walk in the rain with tears streaming down my face, I just wanted to go home and go to bed.

Will dropped me off first, which didn't strike me as unusual until later, and I slept fine and woke up wishing the day would go by quickly so that I could take two different buses and see Daphne again.

Now here I sat with her half a circle away and my hands felt itchy and jittery with the yearning to touch her arm again like I had in the diner.

When her turn came she said she didn't feel like sharing. Everett rarely allowed anybody to take a pass, but her body language screamed: *Leave me alone.*

"Just make sure you seek out help and support if you need it."

She nodded.

I tried to catch her eye. *You okay?*

No luck.

I was last to go and I kept it brief. I'd read an entry on *itainteasybeinoffgreen* about wanting something so badly that you can never have again, something that you must deny yourself forever. When I'd read that earlier in the week, I'd thought of Penny. Now it seemed a little crazy. I had room for more in my life than Penny Brockaway.

Daphne made a quick exit and I slipped out after her.

She speed-walked toward what I knew was her bus stop, her purse swinging wildly at her side, the bracelets on her wrist clanging together. I called after her but she didn't turn around. I didn't run to catch her. From what I'd learned of bus schedules, I had time to spare.

The shelter had no place to sit, so she stood studying a faded, peeling map she knew by heart.

"Daphne," I said.

She didn't turn to face me. "What do you want, River?"

"Are you mad at me?"

"Why would I be mad at you?"

"Because you didn't sit near me."

"Believe it or not, River: everything isn't about you."

"I . . . I don't think everything is about me."

"Really?"

I stretched out my hand to touch her shoulder, but I stopped just short, letting it hover. I thought of diverting to her hair, putting my hand on the back of her neck and taking a fistful of it. "What's wrong? Please. Tell me."

She turned to face me. None of the toughness was gone and yet she looked like she was about to cry.

"My life," she said. "All of it. That's what's wrong."

I wasn't prepared for that. What was I supposed to say? *Your life is great!*

"I think . . . I like you, Daphne," I said.

She laughed, not kindly.

"I mean . . . it turns out I can't stop thinking about you, and when I'm thinking about you I'm not thinking about . . . her."

She stared at me like there was a language barrier or something, eyebrows pulled together, struggling to follow.

"So . . . I've distracted you from the girl you've been crying yourself to sleep over for months—"

"It's only been, like, one month."

"Oh, okay. I see. So it's only been a month."

As much as I didn't want to be thinking about Penny right then, I remembered taking her hand on the sidewalk in front of the house where the lights had just gone out and saying *I'm going to kiss you now,* and remembered her saying *What are you waiting for?*

I reached out and took Daphne's hand. "I'm going to kiss you now," I said.

She yanked her hand away and shoved me hard in the chest. "The hell you are."

"Ow."

"Did that hurt?"

"Sorta."

"Good. Now can you please just go away? I don't need this. Or you."

"Daphne—"

"What?"

"I had a really great time with you last night. Like, the

best time I've had in a long time. And I'm not sure I made that clear."

"Yeah, I know. We went to the dance and we made your girlfriend jealous. It was a big success."

"Daphne—I like you, okay? You."

"You like me?"

"Yes."

"Do you know what I did today, River?"

"No." Crap. I should have called her after the dance. Or texted her. I should have asked her about her day.

"I stole three CDs from Walgreens."

"Why?" I sounded like Natalie.

She laughed. "Because sometimes I just want things to come easy. And sometimes I just can't do everything I'm supposed to."

Again I fought the urge to touch her. "What you did . . . what you do . . . that doesn't change a thing."

"You like me. Why do you like me?"

"Because . . . you're smart. And you're funny. And you're beautiful. And you know more about how the world works than anyone I know. And when I'm with you . . . I . . ."

"You don't think about her?"

"No, I don't. But that's not what I'm trying to say. When I'm with you . . . I want time to slow down."

Just as I said that I heard the gasping sound of the bus's brakes. I turned around and there it was. Its headlights like monster eyes.

"Well, I gotta go."

"Can I ride with you?"

"No. Go home, River."

She stepped onto the bus and swiped her fare card. She turned to look at me.

The doors started to close.

"I like you because of who you are," I blurted out.

She waved her hand at me. Maybe saying good-bye. Maybe brushing me off. Or maybe, I hoped, trying to say that she connected what I'd said to something true inside herself.

THIRTEEN

Why did I still love Penny?

It was an excellent question.

I still loved Penny because that was how I saw myself, as someone who loved Penny Brockaway, and I didn't know how to be somebody different. I still loved Penny because loving her gave my life purpose. I was really, really good at loving Penny. I still loved Penny because I was afraid not to.

After the bus doors closed behind Daphne, I walked back toward A Second Chance. Mason and Christopher stood out on the sidewalk. Christopher blew a plume of smoke in my direction. "What's up with you two?"

"Nothing."

It was clear that neither of them believed me.

"She seemed upset." He grabbed his phone from his sweatshirt pocket and took a few steps away from me. "I'm calling her."

I watched his sneakers as he walked out of earshot—green and black Nike Dunk lows—feeling a sense of shame I didn't understand. What was Daphne going to say to him?

Mason eyed me, shaking his head. "I knew it. I knew there was something about you, River. Something about you that's not right. I mean, don't get me wrong. I like you. I just think you're a liar."

Christopher returned. "I left her a message. Told her to call me if she needs to talk." He glared at me. "Because that's how we do it. Not sure if you got the memo, River, but we come here to help each other through tough times. To listen. Not to try and get laid."

"Or to slum it with a Mexican girl."

"Hey." I took a step closer to Mason. "What's your problem?"

"I throw up my food."

"That's not what I meant."

His big plate of a face went soft. His voice came out at half size. "Sorry, River. But for real. Be honest. Are you into Daphne or what?"

I looked down Pico Boulevard and its string of red lights and decided to tell the truth. "I think maybe I am."

"You can't date her," Christopher said. "You understand that, right? And don't try sleeping with her either."

"That's not what this is about." How to admit to them that after nearly two whole years together Penny and I hadn't ever had sex? Of course I wanted to. But she wasn't ready and that was okay with me. And now she was probably going to have sex with Evan Lockwood, probably already had, and I didn't even know if I cared because nothing made sense anymore.

"What is it about, then?" Mason's tone was gentle.

"I just . . . really like her."

"I really like Daphne too." Christopher stubbed out his half-smoked cigarette and returned it to the pack. "I want to help her stop stealing stuff for no reason because one day she'll land herself in jail. That's just truth. It's one of the many things that make us different. If you or I stole stupid shit, nobody would put us in jail. But Daphne? The same rules don't apply. So she's gotta stop. And if you cared about her you'd focus on that. Not on finding your replacement girlfriend."

"Ugh." Suddenly I hated A Second Chance. I hated the me who went there each week. I wished I'd never walked through its doors.

"Look, River," Mason said. "If you really like Daphne, I mean *really* like her, do her a favor and keep those feelings bottled up somewhere deep inside. That's the right thing to do. It's the only thing to do."

Sunday morning Leonard asked if I wanted to go to the local farmers market with him. What I really wanted to do was stay in my room and do what Penny said I never did—think about things.

We bought tiny carrots and elongated radishes, eggs that had been laid that morning (or so the girl in the flannel shirt said), strawberries, fresh pesto made with arugula and a cinnamon bun for Natalie. All of it an excuse for Leonard to get me alone to talk about one of my least-favorite subjects: my future.

"So . . . just a few more weeks," Leonard said, turning an unidentifiable citrus around in his hand.

"A few more weeks until . . . ?"

He studied me, trying to determine if I was calling his bluff. "Until college acceptance letters come."

"And rejection letters too?"

"River," he sighed. It was only eleven o'clock in the morning and I'd already exasperated him. "You have to want this. It's far too important, too much work and *way* too expensive to stumble your way through it."

"What do you care? It's not like it's costing *you* anything." Damn. Why did I say that?

I tried taking it back. "I'm sorry. I don't mean anything by it. You know I'm really grateful—"

"Stop, River. Please." He turned his back to the citrus stand and faced me. "I know you didn't mean anything by it and I know it's strange that your biological father is paying for college. If I could tell him to take his money and shove it up his ass, I would, believe me, but I can't, and I'm not going to let pride—yours or mine—get in the way of an amazing opportunity for you. And you never, ever, need to tell me you're grateful or thank me for stepping in and acting like a father to you, because it's been one of the greatest privileges of my life."

Leonard had the kindest eyes of anyone I knew, and

over the years, as more wrinkles appeared at their edges, they just got kinder.

"I'm scared about those letters," I said. "I've had about as much rejection as I can take."

"Riv." He put his hand on my shoulder and gave it a squeeze. "You're a great kid. And you've worked hard. You'll have options and you'll choose the place that's right for you. You'll go off to school and you'll continue to work hard and then you'll move back into your bedroom four years later when you can't find a job like all the other college graduates in America."

I laughed. "I'll look forward to that day."

Penny and I had applied to two of the same schools and I'd never seriously considered the others on my list because I figured we'd go together, even though when I mentioned this she looked at me like I was suggesting we run off and join the circus. Penny didn't see me in her future, and I'd never noticed, because I was a fool. Now those two schools were at the bottom of my list. I was done following Penny Brockaway around.

Leonard reached into his wallet to pay the guy behind the stand for a bag of oranges, and as the guy counted out his change I noticed a tattoo on his arm of a tree with roots that disappeared up the sleeve of his white T-shirt.

I took out my phone. "Excuse me . . . would you mind if I took a picture of your tattoo?"

He stuck his arm out and held it patiently as I took several shots using different filters.

Leonard watched me, baffled.

"It's just a hobby," I said as we walked away. "Don't worry."

I texted the best of the shots, the one with the bluish retro filter, to Daphne.

Me: U like?

Her:

When we got back home I went to my room and booted up my laptop. After I'd checked out a few websites I stalked for sneaker bargains, my fingers hovered above my keyboard and though I willed them not to, they typed: *Thaddeus Dean.*

I didn't want to care what my father looked like. Where he lived and worked. What he'd been doing. What he'd written, what others wrote about him. I wanted to believe that he didn't matter, that I was okay without him, better even. I didn't want to wonder what he'd make of me. Almost eighteen years old. About to go off to college and start a life that he was underwriting.

His face filled my screen.

Still with a close-cropped beard. Still with those square-framed glasses. I don't know what I expected—it hadn't been that long since I'd looked him up—but I always braced for a shock.

I scrolled through some pictures. On a stage giving a speech at South by Southwest. A head shot that appeared in the upper corner of an article he wrote called "Internet Integrity and Expanding Global Reach." And a black-and-white photograph of him in a suit, standing next to a brick wall, used in a flyer for an upcoming conference on Interconnectedness and Conflict Resolution at the Barton Center in . . . Santa Monica.

It made no sense that this hit me like a kick to the nuts. Over the years Thaddeus Dean had probably come in and out of town dozens of times. It wasn't like I lived in Omaha. I knew he never tried to see me when he came. I also knew that if he wanted, he could find me in the digital world any day of the year, and he never did.

I closed my laptop and tried to erase the date and time of his appearance from my consciousness, but it was like trying to unsee something you wished you'd never seen, like your parents having sex or something. The more you pretend you didn't see it, the deeper the burn on your memory.

Natalie was off at a birthday party or else I'd have taken her to do something—maybe a pony ride at the Country Mart—even though she was a good year or two past pony rides.

Mom and Leonard were in the kitchen chopping up some of our farmers market haul. There was barely room for the two of them in there, but they'd learned how to keep from bumping up against each other.

"I'm going out," I said.

"Where are you going, honey?"

I didn't want to say *I don't know* because I knew that

would make Mom worry and maybe try to have another talk with me about my feelings so I said, "It's such a gorgeous day, I thought I'd take a walk."

Mom and Leonard exchanged a smile. "Great. That's just great. Have a great time."

I waited for the bus heading west. I knew how to get to mid-Pico and back home again, but I'd never ridden the bus in the other direction. After an eternity it finally arrived and I hopped on and slipped the driver my fare.

I stared out the window without paying much attention and before I knew it the temperature had dropped a few degrees and the air smelled of salt. I got off and found a coffee shop with a big patio where lots of guys sat shirtless with girls in bikini tops, dogs tied out front near surfboards and bikes. Since getting sun for me meant turning a shade somewhere on the spectrum between pink and red, I chose a table indoors and ordered an iced latte. The girl who made it for me had a tattoo of a strawberry on one forearm and a pineapple on the other. The guy who took my money had LUCY tattooed on his bicep. This was Venice Beach, where not having a tattoo was as good as forgetting to wear pants.

The idea came to me halfway through my latte.

I went back to the guy who'd taken my money. He seemed more than happy to let me snap a picture, though I had to get really close because I wanted separate photos of the *L* and the *C*.

I wandered around the patio and pretty quickly found the other letters I was looking for: an *M* in your typical

MOM tattoo inside a heart with an arrow and the *A* and the *E* in a long quote that ran between the shoulder blades of a beautiful girl's back.

I sent each photograph of a tattooed letter in a separate text in quick succession.

C-A-L-L-M-E

I sat back and waited, but my phone didn't ring until I was on the bus again, halfway home.

"Cute," she said when I picked up.

"Cute? I thought you said my work should be shown in a gallery."

"Why are you talking funny?"

"Because I'm on the bus."

"Riding the bus. Look who's all grown up."

"Daphne, I—"

"Wait. Just be quiet for a minute."

"Okay." It was easy enough because I wasn't sure what I wanted to say. The bus stopped and started, inching its way east in postbeach Sunday traffic.

"I'm sorry I was weird last night."

"You don't—"

"Will you let me finish? Jeez, River. You're like a girl. You can't stop talking."

"Sorry."

"I'm mad at myself. For wanting to do things I know I shouldn't do. Sometimes just keeping from doing those things can be totally exhausting. You must understand, right? Like, it's probably that way with you and weed."

"Yeah, I guess."

"And I don't have time or room in my life to like a boy."

By *boy* I really, really hoped she meant me.

"And there are so many reasons I shouldn't like you, River. For one thing, you're white. Like superduper white. And you live on the Westside. And you're a marijuana addict. And you conceal your addiction from your friends. And I'm pretty sure you're still hung up on another girl. And you don't even drive. I could go on and on, but I only have, like, seven hundred minutes on my cell plan. But the thing is, I feel like I can trust you and that I know you better than I do, which is sort of scary. It makes me want to find the room and the time because I feel . . . good when I'm with you." A few beats of silence. "You're allowed to say something now."

"Now?"

"Yes, now. Go."

"Okay. I don't want it to feel like we know each other better than we do. I want us to know each other for real. Not in a high school way." I saw that my stop was coming up, but I didn't pull the cord. "I . . . I want to be your friend. I want to be a true friend. That's . . . probably more important than anything else right now."

"So . . . what was up with that whole *I'm going to kiss you now* bullshit?"

"Oh, I do want to kiss you. Like, I really, *really* want to kiss you. But I also want to listen to you. I want to . . . help you. If, like, you need to talk about why you steal, how it's unfair that you can't have all the things you deserve."

She sighed.

I dug my fingertips into my eyes. Pushed until I saw bursts of color.

"Where you at now?" she asked.

I looked out the window. "Somewhere east of my house. I missed my stop."

"Get off at Crenshaw."

"Then what?"

"There's a Pizza Hut on the corner. Wait for me there."

Just as it started to sink in that she wasn't going to show—that I'd hopped off that bus, jumped when she said "Jump," just like I did with Penny—I looked up and there she was.

"Hi."

"Hi."

We stood face to face on a busy and not-so-beautiful street corner with the smells of a Pizza Hut wafting over us. No magical streetlamp like where I first took Penny Brockaway's face in my hands and kissed her.

I took a step closer, not sure what to do or say. Wishing it was as easy as it had been that night with Penny, but knowing this was different, more complicated and more real.

But she stepped back. "You want to eat something?"

"No."

"You got something against Pizza Hut?"

"I have everything against Pizza Hut."

She smiled. "Me too. Come on."

We walked back to the bus stop just as a bus was pulling

up. I grabbed her hand and led her down the near-empty aisle to two seats in the last row. She draped one leg over mine and I put my hand on her knee. We sat as close as two people could without sharing the same seat.

"Where are we going?" I asked.

"Nowhere."

"I didn't mean metaphorically."

She laughed and leaned even closer. "Sometimes I ride the bus just to get some room to think. And I like to watch people. Imagine them—the secrets they keep. The stuff they can't admit. I wonder . . . what would this person do if she could do anything? If there were no walls or boundaries, what would that guy do? What would happen to their lives if this bus granted wishes?"

I stared at her. I think it had been a while since I'd blinked. I knew she was inviting me to look around, but I couldn't take my eyes off her.

"Daphne—"

"Take this one here." She nodded at a slight woman a few rows up to our left whose seat faced the aisle. She wore a jacket too heavy for the weather and her feet were encircled by shopping bags. "What do you think?"

"I think she looks tired and sad."

"Remember, this bus grants wishes."

"Right." Her hair covered most of her face and she hadn't looked up from her hands in her lap. "Last night she won five hundred bucks in a karaoke competition, enough for a plane ticket to New York. She wants to audition for a Broadway musical. She's been saving up, putting away every dollar she can manage into an empty tampon box she keeps under the bathroom sink."

"Ha." Daphne took my hand, the one that rested on her knee, and laced her fingers through mine.

"She gets the part, by the way. And then she wins a Tony."

Daphne looked at the woman, who still hadn't looked up from her lap, and smiled. "Do you want to know what wishes I have that I don't admit?"

"Of course I do."

"I want to be a lawyer. I want to do immigration or maybe workers' rights. Does that sound crazy?"

"Why would it sound crazy?"

"Because I've already been on the wrong side of the law. And I'll need another three years of school on top of college. That's a lot of dollars I'd have to hide in my tampon box."

I squeezed her hand. "I believe in you. I know that's one of those things people say, but I mean it. You've got what it takes to do whatever you dream of."

She moved her face an inch closer to mine. "This *is* the bus that grants wishes. Where anybody can be anything."

"Yes it is."

"And on this bus, maybe it doesn't matter that our group has rules or that we're from different places or that we both have a crapload of problems."

I took my index finger and touched it to her bottom lip.

Now didn't seem like a good time to tell her I wasn't addicted to marijuana; that if I could be whoever I wanted

I'd be the boy who never lied. I wasn't sure when it would ever feel like the right time to tell her the truth, but I knew it wasn't now when all I could think about was kissing her.

Which I did. Quickly, just as our magic bus reached the end of the line.

FOURTEEN

Before Penny, nobody had spent much time gossiping about me, and that was how it was after she dumped me. But now that I'd brought a mystery girl to the dance I became a person of interest again. People were talking about me and *that girl*.

After weeks sitting rows away in Spanish class, Penny moved in next to me.

"Hey, River." She gave me a little wave right as Mr. Fernandez cleared his throat and said *Buenos dias, amigos*. I gave her an apologetic shrug.

Penny always took forever to gather her things after class—each pencil, each eraser had a precise spot—but when I jumped up she shoveled everything into her bag and followed me out into the hallway.

"Hey," she said.

"Hey."

"Did you have fun Friday night?"

"Yeah. It was fun."

"Great. Yeah, I had fun too."

"Okay, then." I turned to walk toward my locker.

"River," she said.

"Yeah?"

She bit her upper lip. "This is weird."

"Yeah, I know." I almost reached out and took her hand, but only because that was what I used to do when she needed some reassurance.

"I just don't want things to be weird between us."

Well then, maybe you shouldn't have dumped me in the middle of the lake.

"Okay . . ."

"So, we're good?"

"Yeah, we're good."

"Because I care about you, River. And I want us to be friends."

Luke and I had lunch period together and we sat out near the football field splitting a bag of Cool Ranch Doritos.

"What's up with Will and Maggie?" he asked.

"What do you mean?"

"Well, they didn't call me back all weekend. Neither did you, but I'm used to that. Anyway, I wanted to see what those guys were up to 'cause I didn't have plans after the game, but they didn't call or text or anything. So then I find out they went to the movies and I ask Will this morning which one they saw, and he smiles and says he can't remember."

"Hold on to your briefs, but I think they might be into each other."

"Duh. When I asked *what's up with them* I meant *are they finally getting it on.*"

"What? You knew?"

"It's been obvious since forever."

"It has?"

"River. Dude. You're kind of clueless."

I ate the last few Doritos, going over Friday night again. The way Maggie looked. The way Will noticed the way she looked.

"So . . . tell me more about the dance," Luke said.

"I thought you hated dances."

"I do, but it doesn't mean I don't want to hear about them after the fact."

"Penny and Evan were together. But you already knew that."

"Yeah." He took a long sip from his soda.

"Do you know more?"

"When nobody called me back I ended up going out with Evan and some of the other guys from the team after the game."

"And?"

"You want me to tell you about Evan and Penny?"

I thought about this. "Not really."

"Good. So why don't you tell me about this girl you brought."

"She's Mexican."

"So you think I might know her? Because I'm half Mexican? Do you think maybe we're cousins?"

"No, asshole. I was just telling you about her because you asked. She's Mexican. She lives in Boyle Heights. She's smart as anything and she confuses the hell out of me, which I like. Her name is Daphne."

"Daphne. That has a good sound to it. It sounds so . . ."

"So . . . not Penny?"

"Yes."

"Was I really that bad when I was with Penny?"

He sighed. "Sorta. It was like the way my dad likes to tell the same story over and over again. It's not that there's anything wrong with the story, it's just that you get really tired of hearing it."

"I get it." Everett had this thing he'd make us do when we'd hurt someone's feelings, but I wasn't about to look at Luke and say "I honor you" because Luke would probably have thought I was having a stroke and called an ambulance. But I did tap him so he turned to look me in the eye when I said what I needed to say.

"I'm sorry if I haven't been a good friend."

He narrowed his eyes. "You aren't about to give me a pair of short-shorts, are you?"

I laughed. "No. You in those shorts is high on the list of things I never want to see."

I approached Penny after Spanish class Wednesday in the hall. She'd said she wanted to be friends and I took her at her word.

"Hey, Pen."

"Hi, River." Those two words sounded so different than when she'd found me on her back steps with her dog, or in her kitchen with Natalie. Then she'd said hello in a way that meant: *What the hell are you doing at my house?* This time, she sounded pleased to see me.

"I didn't do my homework," I said.

"Why not?"

I thought of telling her about how Daphne had called last night after she got everyone to bed and we'd stayed on the phone until 1 a.m. I didn't want to tell Penny this to make her jealous, but because I couldn't concentrate on math or Spanish or anything ordinary: Daphne was an electric distraction.

"I just didn't have the time."

She leaned in close. "Don't tell anyone," she whispered. "But I had Juana do my homework."

I guessed Juana didn't particularly enjoy that task, but I also guessed she did it without complaint. Probably right after cooking Penny's family a bland meal.

"So . . ."

This "so . . ." meant she'd heard that things between me and the girl from the dance were maybe going somewhere. I wasn't sure how. I hadn't told anyone I'd kissed Daphne. That was a good secret in the midst of so many others that weren't so great.

"So?"

"Come on, River."

I'd have kept playing dumb, but I knew that if there was

something Penny wanted, she wouldn't quit until she got it. Especially when she wanted that something from me.

"Oh, so you mean you want to know about the girl?"

"Maybe."

"Well, there's this girl. And I like her. And it turns out she just might like me too, because . . . the world is a mysterious and unpredictable place."

"Is she, like, your girlfriend now?"

"It's more complicated than that."

"What's so complicated?"

I shrugged. How could I say that getting to know Daphne was a whole different endeavor than getting to know Penny? If I'd ever even really known Penny in the first place.

"Well, I'm happy for you." She didn't sound it.

"And Evan?"

"Yeah . . . I don't know. . . ." She took down her hair from its bun, shook it out, and started to redo it. "I'm not sure I really want to be in a relationship right now. College letters come soon, and I have to decide where I'm going and think about my future and it's just sort of weird starting over with someone else. Getting to know someone and all that. It's so much work, don't you think?"

No, I didn't. It felt like the opposite of work.

"I guess so."

"It's the end of our senior year, Riv." She looked at me the way she used to, right before telling me what I needed to do, or wear, or say. "It's just not the time to start something new."

FiFTEEN

From Everett's yellow pamphlet, page one, bullet point two:

> • *A SECOND CHANCE support group for teens is built on trust, on the understanding that there are no lies, no hidden truths.*

I understood this and willingly violated it week after week. And now Daphne, who didn't pretend to be someone she wasn't, who respected Everett and his rules, grappled with the uncomfortable truth that she was violating page two, bullet point four:

> • *No physical or romantic relationships between group members.*

"Being honest in there is really important," she told me between kisses. "But I just don't think everyone needs to know everything."

"Being honest is important to me too," I heard myself say.

"I know it is, River. It's one of the reasons I like you. And one of the reasons I can see us together."

"I thought it was my quick wit and unmatched charm."

I hadn't been able to wait until Saturday. I didn't want to share her with a roomful of addicts. So on Friday I begged her to meet me at a movie. We only made it through the first twenty minutes, after which we left to buy popcorn and never returned. I didn't want to watch a movie; I wanted to watch her. We sat out in the empty lobby.

"Yeah, that, and you understand my problems and I get yours. We're a broken set."

"A broken set. I like that."

"What about Christopher and Mason?" She took a piece of popcorn and tossed it in the air, catching it in her mouth. "Maybe we should tell them."

"Well, Christopher is overprotective of you, and we all know what a big mouth Mason has."

"That's rude."

"What?"

"Making fun of someone with an eating disorder."

"I wasn't making fun of him. I was saying, literally, Mason has a big mouth."

"No, River, you weren't saying *literally* he has a big mouth, like he's a Pac-Man or some shit. You were saying it *figuratively,* but I'll give you the benefit of the doubt that you were talking about his gossiping and not his eating."

Man, I thought. *I could really fall in love with this girl.*

The next night we met out front. I got there first and stood with everyone until Daphne arrived and greeted us casually, like there wasn't one among us who'd been counting the minutes until he could kiss her again.

We sat together at the far end of the circle. I spent the whole meeting sweating that I'd somehow out us, make an amateur mistake, forgetting that I'd become a world-class liar.

It was Daphne's turn.

"It's been . . . a pretty amazing week." She smiled at Christopher, who sat across from her, like he was the reason. "All the work . . . none of it felt like a burden, you know? Like I didn't really mind. And I think that's because for the first time in a really long time I'm doing something for myself. Just for me. I know I come here, and that's something for me, but I mean something that makes me excited and happy. That's maybe what the shoplifting is about. . . . I don't know . . . maybe it's about taking something nice for myself. Maybe that's why I steal stuff I don't even care about. Because I'm trying to take something for *me*. I don't mean that to sound like an excuse, I'm just trying to understand it better. That's part of this whole process, right?"

Hand gestures back and forth.

"And I know we're here to share or whatever, but I feel like keeping this to myself, you know, keeping it . . . just for me."

"That's okay, Daphne," Everett said. "Not every piece

of ourselves must be shared. So long as what you keep secret isn't feeding your addiction."

It was my turn to speak, but Everett's last sentence stopped me cold. *So long as what you keep secret isn't feeding your addiction.*

Was Daphne Vargas, my new and beautiful secret, feeding my addiction? Was I addicted to having a girlfriend? To being loved? Was I incurably needy? Was that why I couldn't even be honest with the girl I was falling in love with about who I really was? Did I even know who I really was?

I took a deep breath. Tried clearing my head. I couldn't pose the questions that flooded me, and I couldn't just sit there saying nothing. I shifted in my seat, and my chair made one of those noises that hurt inside your teeth.

This is it, I thought. *This is what it's like for every other member of the group. This is what it feels like to come here and wrestle with something real.*

Everyone waited. We'd all become experts in the art of patience.

I wanted to say something. I wanted to speak as me, not as that nameless Midwestern kid with a blog and an addiction to weed. Not the liar and the faker. Not the impostor. I wanted to be honest. I remembered Everett's directive from a few weeks back:

Tell us something real. Tell us something true.

"I don't need marijuana," I said. "I'm not an addict." It was my opener, but I didn't know how to follow it up. The room stayed quiet.

"So that's it," Mason finally said through a fake smile. "You just gave up weed. See how easy that was? Bam! Up in smoke!" He waved at me. "You can go now. Have a nice life."

"What I think Mason is trying to say"—Everett shot Mason a disapproving look—"is that you may not believe you need marijuana anymore, but addictions don't disappear, we just get better at controlling them. You'll always be an addict, even though you can be a healthy person. Don't forget that."

Forget it? It was all I thought about. *How the hell do I shake this fake marijuana addiction?*

That night we went back to Philippe's—just Christopher and Daphne and me. Mason opted out. I sat across from Daphne in the booth. If I sat next to her I wouldn't be able to keep from touching her.

Christopher reached for one of my potato chips. "Mason sure has it out for you."

"Yeah . . . I don't know. Maybe he's right about me. Maybe I do have it too easy," I said.

"Well . . . weed is kind of a lame vice."

"River." Daphne stared at me. "Your dad abandoned you. He just up and left you. I don't care if you think you don't care. If you think your life is fine because you have a nice stepfather now and a house in Rancho Park. You're an abandoned child. Stop thinking you have it so easy."

You know how when the Grinch hears the Whos down

in Whoville singing, his small heart grows three sizes? Well, it wasn't my heart; it was that stupid frog inside me. It grew into an enormous beast. I couldn't say a thing.

Christopher drew his hands up to his chest. "Awww. I'm moved that River opens up to you privately. Because I certainly haven't heard that sob story about his abandonment. I'm glad you two have that kind of . . . intimate relationship."

Daphne kicked his shin under the table. "Shut up, Christopher."

"Why so defensive?"

"Look," she said. "I'm sick of the innuendo. If you want to know what's going on with River and me, just ask."

"Okay. I'm asking. What's going on with River and you?"

She looked at me and then at Christopher. "Absolutely nothing."

When we pulled up to Daphne's house, I got out of the car and held the door for her. I gave her a hug and tried to imprint in my sensory bank the quick kiss I landed on her cheek, because I didn't go to school with Daphne, she didn't live in a huge house walking distance from mine, she didn't have an SUV at her disposal—I didn't know when I'd see her next.

She hugged me back and whispered, "Good night, *guapo.*"

On the ramp onto the 10 West Christopher said, "For

the record: she's totally into you. I don't care what she says."

"No she's not."

"I don't know why she'd like some skinny white boy from Rancho Park, but she does. I can tell."

I just let the words sit there.

We pulled in front of my house and I said I'd see him next week. But I wasn't certain I'd go. I wanted to. I even felt like I *needed* it. But how much longer could I fake my addiction?

The irony wasn't lost on me that I didn't know how to get clean.

I walked into the house full of agitation that Mom sniffed out right away.

"You okay, honey?"

"I'm fine."

"Everything all right?"

"Everything is perfect."

"Nothing is perfect, River. Don't let perfect be the enemy of good."

"Ah, yoga wisdom." I put my palms together and did a little bow. *"Namaste."*

I avoided Leonard's disapproving glare. I wasn't even sure why I was being a dick to Mom other than that my agitation was growing like those tiny toy sponges you drop in water and watch turn into dinosaurs and seahorses, or in Natalie's most recent set, flowers and hearts. I couldn't help but think that maybe the best way to combat this feeling was to smoke a big fat joint. Getting my hands on pot wasn't a problem. Everyone at school knew who dealt pot. Maybe if I bought a whole bunch I could smoke it every day and develop a real addiction—become the person I pretended to be.

My phone buzzed in my pocket.

When I saw that it was Daphne, that agitation vanished like a magic trick, and calmness settled in, like I had just smoked that nonexistent joint or maybe done some of Mom's yoga poses.

Her: Family picnic next Saturday. My brother Miguel is turning 10.

Me: K

Her: I want u to come.

Me: K

Her: K?

Me: K!

Her: Carne asada on the grill. And maybe some softball. How do u feel about piñatas?

Me: I'm against violence of any kind.

Her: It's some Minecraft character who probably deserves it.

Me: In that case, I'll bring my bat.

SIXTEEN

Wrong as I knew it was, I started to fantasize that after Daphne's final two mandatory meetings, neither of us would go anymore, and that we'd spend our future Saturday nights together doing what high school seniors do: going to parties, hanging out with friends, maybe drinking a little, but never, ever smoking any weed.

I knew the meetings helped Daphne. They were valuable to her. But if we stopped going I'd never have to tell her or the rest of the group the truth. We could start over. *The Girl Who Doesn't Steal and the Boy Who Doesn't Smoke Pot Meet Unexpectedly and Fall Madly in Love.* Even I wanted to watch that romantic comedy.

But I didn't want Daphne to step away from something that meant so much to her. I was starting to fall in love, and I wanted to do it right.

I had to come clean. Mom's yoga wisdom had it right. *Don't let perfect be the enemy of good.* I wasn't, couldn't, be the perfect boyfriend. I'd made too many mistakes. Told too many lies. But I needed to show Daphne that even though I wasn't perfect, I was still good enough.

Luke picked me up for school Monday morning. Will and Maggie sat in the backseat, where the ungodly hour didn't prevent them from having their hands all over each other.

"So this is out in the open? Are we done pretending it isn't happening? Was there a confessional moment I missed?"

Maggie untwined herself from Will. "You sorta miss out on all the moments, River."

She was right. I'd missed too much. Of everything. That was something I didn't want to do anymore.

"I'm happy for you guys," I said. "And Will, no offense, but Maggie was my friend first, she taught me how to do my makeup, so, you know, I'll have to kill you if you do anything to hurt her."

He smiled.

We pulled into the parking lot and I grabbed my backpack out of Luke's trunk. Will took Maggie's hand and we started up toward the main building.

"So where were you Saturday night?" Luke asked me. "You missed the lamest party of the decade."

"I was with Daphne."

"Of course," Will said. "Where else would you be?"

"Listen, guys." I stopped to face them. "Things are going to be different with Daphne than they were with Penny. *I'm* going to be different with Daphne than I was with Penny. Promise. I've been getting help. Working on my stuff."

"Getting help?" Maggie asked. "You're seeing a shrink?"

"Sort of."

"Don't be embarrassed, River. Look around you. At least nine-tenths of the kids at our school see shrinks."

"I'm not embarrassed. It's just—"

"What?" They stopped in the middle of the steps. The bell was about to ring. I thought of the woman Mom made me see when I was little, the one with the smudgy glasses who reeked of patchouli. The one I kept asking why I didn't have a dad to cheer from the soccer sidelines. "It's just that she smells like patchouli."

In Spanish class that week Penny sat next to me every single day, taking the whole *I want us to be friends* thing to a new level. I wanted to be friends with Penny too. How could I not? Penny used to be the person I thought about all the time. The person I wanted to call when I saw something funny on TV or when Mom said one of her ridiculous old person-y things, like when she held her phone at arm's length and said she was taking a facie instead of a selfie, or especially when I saw a wounded animal. Wounded animals were of particular interest to Penny, except when that wounded animal was me and she didn't seem all that interested, until now when I wasn't so wounded anymore.

And I needed a friend. Sure, three best friends is more than most people have, but I couldn't tell Maggie, Will or Luke the truth. Doing that would mean admitting I'd failed them like I'd failed everyone else.

And Penny? She was like a new friend. Someone I was just getting to know. In a way, our slate was clean. I hadn't betrayed her. I didn't owe her a thing. For all these reasons, I thought about confiding in Penny.

On Thursday she asked if I'd walk her home because her car was getting fixed and I said sure because she was my friend now, and I had nothing better to do.

"How come you don't come by anymore?" she asked when we were a few blocks from school.

"Because you told me not to."

"Oh yeah. Well, it was kind of weird at first, you know? Like you weren't really getting the message that we were over?" She laughed.

I thought: *This is funny?*

"My mom was, like, kind of freaked out that you kept showing up. She told Juana not to let you in the house!"

More laughter.

Really? This is sidesplitting humor?

"But we're friends now, so you should feel free to come over and text me or whatever, anytime."

"Okay."

We passed the deli where I'd bought her chicken soup. A quart of chicken soup goes for $12.95—not an insignificant amount of money. She'd never thanked me for it. I wondered if she ever even drank it or if she just dumped it down the kitchen sink.

"Did you notice I finally got that surgery?" She batted her eyelashes at me.

"I didn't. But I couldn't ever tell when you were wearing contacts anyway. And since you'd never be caught dead with your glasses at school . . ."

"I know, right? I looked hideous in those glasses."

"Not true."

"Come on. I looked heinous."

"Hideous *and* heinous?"

"And horrifying."

"You looked cute in your glasses. I've told you that before."

"Yeah. You were always so sweet to me. I don't know why I didn't appreciate you more."

"I didn't feel underappreciated."

"You didn't?"

"Not until you dumped me."

More laughter. She linked her arm through mine.

We were on her block now and I hadn't had a chance to broach the subject of the big stinking hole of lies I'd dug myself into, because Penny hadn't asked me about my life, because Penny and I weren't really friends, and we probably never would be.

"This is nice," she said.

We walked up her front steps and Penny reached around in her backpack for her keys, then smacked herself on the forehead. "Duh. My keys are with my car in the shop."

She rang the doorbell.

I didn't really want to go inside. What were we supposed to do as friends? We weren't going to curl up on the couch and watch a movie. I wasn't going to try to make out with her. And I definitely wasn't going to tell her about my problems.

Juana opened the door. When I saw the look on her face as she took me and Penny in, I knew it was time to leave.

"Hi, River." She didn't move aside to let us in. "Um. Penelope? Your mother, she said that I'm not to let—"

"It's okay, Juana."

"But your mother, she said—"

"It's okay, Juana. I invited River over. He's totally not stalking me anymore."

"But—"

"Juana. Let us in. This is silly. It's just River. You know River. Does he look like a psychopath to you?"

"No, but—"

"It's okay," I said, though everything felt far from okay. Uncomfortable, embarrassed and awkward? Yes. Okay? No. "I need to get going."

"No, River." Penny took me by the hand and tugged. "Come inside."

"I'm going to go." I slipped my hand out of Penny's and saw her narrow her eyes at Juana.

"I'm sorry, River," Juana said. "You know I think you're a nice boy. It's just that—"

"It's okay, Juana. Thanks. You're just doing what Mrs. Brockaway told you to do. I understand."

Penny turned her narrow eyes to me. "Well, I'm telling her to let you inside. This is stupid."

"I gotta go." I turned around and started walking quickly down the driveway.

"I'm really sorry, River," Juana called out after me. "You take care now."

SEVENTEEN

Daphne was busy helping set up Miguel's party so she suggested I try taking the Metro to Boyle Heights.

I'd always thought of an LA subway system as a little like flying cars—a fantasy that would never come to pass. But it existed; it just didn't service the Westside world I knew, so just like the bus, I figured nobody ever rode it.

I had Leonard drive me to the Red Line station at Vermont Avenue. It was way too far a walk from my house, farther even than A Second Chance.

"So what's at the other end of your subway ride?" he asked me.

"A girl."

"I figured."

"You did?"

"Why else does a boy put on his best button-down shirt on a Saturday morning?"

"To be fair, it's sorta my only one."

"The day I met your mother I was wearing a mock turtleneck."

"Good thing she was never exactly fashion forward."

He laughed. "She was nothing like any of the women I'd ever dated, and she had a bratty little boy to boot! But oh man. Did I fall hard." Leonard pulled up to the curb and peered at the subway entrance. "I've always wanted to take the Metro."

"So what's stopped you?"

He shrugged. "Life, I guess."

"If I could drive I wouldn't be taking the Metro either."

"So what's stopped you from getting your license?"

"Life, I guess."

He pulled out his wallet and handed me a twenty-dollar bill. I tried shooing him away but he pressed it into my palm and squeezed my hand. "Have fun today, kiddo. Call me if you need anything."

I switched from the red to the gold train at Union Station and got out at Mariachi Plaza, where Daphne was meeting me to drive me to the park. I took the escalator up from the platform holding a gift for Miguel.

I'd enlisted Natalie's help. Even though I knew that an eight-year-old-girl and a ten-year-old boy are practically different species, Natalie was a keen observer of people, and I figured she might have a sense of what boys were into these days.

"I know he likes Minecraft."

"Ugh. Minecraft. So boring."

"So what should I get him?"

"What about a pet?"

"That might be a bit much."

"A small pet. Like a lizard or a fish. Everyone likes pets."

"Uh, I don't think so, Nat. What else does everyone like that doesn't require care and keeping?"

"Pens."

"Pens?"

"Yeah. Everyone likes nice pens. Like a set of ones you can draw with, you know, with different-sized tips and stuff."

So I bought Miguel some pens and a book of art paper and I spent the ride over to Mariachi Plaza working up a healthy sweat that I'd picked out the totally wrong gift because it was easier to worry about the pens than it was to worry that Daphne's extended family would hate me.

I came out of the depths of the station into sunlight reflected through a collection of diamond-shaped stained-glass panels stretching out above my head. I looked up. The panels formed a wing, an eagle wing or maybe an angel wing in a nod to our city, a beautiful architectural detail. I saw Daphne, standing in front of me, bathed in multicolored light. She smiled and I thought:

HERE: Is Daphne in a rainbow.

THIS: Is what happiness looks like.

NOW: I need to kiss her.

She examined the gift. "What you got there?"

"It's for Miguel."

"The wrapping paper with balloons was sort of a give-away."

"It's pens. And paper. Nice pens. And nice enough paper."

She nodded. "Good choice."

"Are you just trying to make me feel better?"

"No. He'll love it. He's big into drawing comics."

"Whew." As we walked from the square to her car holding hands, the knot in my stomach only grew tighter.

"You're nervous."

"That obvious?"

"Well, holding your hand feels kind of like holding an eel."

I pulled my hand away and wiped it on my jeans. "Have you spent a lot of time holding eels?"

"Only nervous ones."

We arrived at her car and she unlocked the doors. We rolled down the windows because it was roughly two hundred degrees inside.

"Just so you know . . . I haven't told anyone you're coming."

"Why not?"

"It just seemed easier to show up with you than to try and explain you."

"I guess."

I leaned my head out the window a little and let the hot air whip me in the face. Daphne was a good driver, as far as someone who doesn't drive can tell. I began to relax a little. I leaned back into my seat. We waited at a red light and I took in her profile, this girl with whom I was falling in love. Her radiant skin and big dark eyes. Her thick, lush hair. I reached out to touch it just as we took a turn to the right, a little abruptly, and the figurine hanging from her rearview mirror swung into my path. I caught it and turned it over in my hand.

St. Jude.

The patron saint of lost causes.

"Oh my God." I turned and looked in the backseat, whipped back around to check out the dashboard. I stuck my head out the window again to get a look at the car's exterior. Dark green.

"What?"

"This is your car?"

"It's my mom's car. Why?"

I reached out and grabbed that saint again. Daphne drove another block and pulled over. I jumped out and ran around to the back: a bumper sticker for the radio station I'd never listened to. I didn't need to go to the front of the car to see if the left bumper was smashed in because I already knew: this was Juana's car. The car I'd never bothered to notice because I'd never bothered to think about Juana's life beyond her role as a maid. I'd never stopped to wonder if Juana might have a family of her own, a daughter who had to fend for herself and her siblings Monday through Friday so that her mother could cater to Penny Brockaway's every need.

"What's going on?" Daphne watched in confusion as I paced a circle around the car, probably the same way

I looked at Penny when she said to me in the middle of Echo Park Lake: "I can't do this anymore."

I could try that line right now. I could say to Daphne *I can't do this anymore*. I could walk away. I could forget her, forget everything, forget this entire mess that just kept getting messier. If I went home now Daphne would return to the party upset, and maybe Juana would ask her what was wrong and she'd tell her about this boy named River and how he'd disappointed her by turning out to be just another bad choice.

River, the boy with the unforgettable name.

You're a nice boy, River. You have a kind heart. I know this about you.

What were the odds? In a city of almost four million people. What were the goddamn odds?

The connections in my brain only sizzled and smoked.

Daphne started walking toward the baseball diamond. Balloons. Plastic tablecloths. Party hats. A piñata hanging from a tree branch. I could smell the lighter fluid from the barbecue.

"Daphne, wait."

I caught up to her at the fence behind home plate. She looked at me with her last bit of patience.

"There's something I have to tell you . . . I love you. Okay? I really do. I love you, Daphne." She smiled and it almost knocked my legs right out from under me. "But that's not what I need to tell you. What I need to say . . . this is super awkward and sort of unbelievable and I'm not sure how—"

"River?"

I didn't have to turn to see who'd said my name. I knew her voice. I'd heard that voice say my name for nearly two whole years.

Daphne looked over my shoulder. "Mom?"

"Daphne? River?" The voice was drawing nearer. I still didn't turn to face Juana. I took Daphne's hand. "What I was trying to tell you. Your mom. I just realized I know your mom. This is so crazy, but—"

"River?" I turned around. Juana stared at me from the other side of the chain link fence. "River. What are you doing here?"

Daphne dropped my hand and looked at me, at her mom, and back at me again. "I don't understand."

"Why are you here, River? Penelope isn't here. Why are *you* here?"

"Penelope? What does Penelope . . ." Daphne stopped. Her mouth hung open. "Oh. My. God."

I couldn't form a coherent sentence so I just stood there while the two of them looked at me.

"River. You don't belong here. Why'd you come today?"

"Mom. River is sort of like my boyfriend."

"No, River is Penelope's boyfriend. But Penelope doesn't like River anymore. And River keeps coming to the house even when Mrs. Brockaway says he's not allowed inside."

"You still go to her house?"

"I . . . I . . . I don't go there anymore."

"You came two days ago."

"Shit." I knew Juana hated swearing, she always scolded

Penny and Ben when they used bad language. "I'm sorry. I mean . . ."

"I think you should go," Daphne said.

"No, wait. Let me explain. . . . I didn't know."

"You didn't know what?"

"I didn't know you were Juana's daughter. I swear."

"Wait . . . is this why you starting coming to the meetings in the first place? Did you think knowing me could get you closer to her?"

"River goes to your meetings? River? Are you in trouble for stealing too?"

"No, Mom. River is addicted to marijuana."

"Oh. That's bad, River. Mrs. Brockaway said something was wrong with you, but I didn't know it was drugs."

"Oh, Jesus." That wasn't any better than saying *shit* in Juana's book. I knew this, but I somehow couldn't stop myself.

I took a step closer to Daphne and said, "I'm not an addict. I pretended to be because I liked the meetings and then I liked you."

She looked at me like a stranger, or worse, because she wouldn't have reason to hate a total stranger. "You need to go," she said.

"But—"

"Now."

I held the present out to her. "Please. Give this to Miguel."

She shoved it back at me. "I don't ever want to see you

again." She turned and walked away, toward the gate that opened into the park.

Juana still stood near home plate, on the other side of the fence, but I could feel her anger like there was no barrier at all between us. "You go home, River. Don't come back here. Or to Penelope's. You just stay away. You understand me?"

EIGHTEEN

Needless to say, I didn't go to A Second Chance that night. I stayed home, feverish with shame and regret. I wanted to go to the meeting; I ached to go to the meeting, because as it turned out, I needed it. More than the soup Mom made to combat my phony illness, or the handmade card Natalie slipped under my door: *Feel better soon, River Dean/Marks. Love, your favorite sister.*

Yes, I wanted to see Daphne and I wanted to straighten out this huge mess I'd made, I wanted to fix things between us, but I also wanted to sit in that room with that group of people and talk about the hardest part of my week, which had happened earlier that very day, and I wanted to say out loud so that everyone could hear, *I'M A ROYAL SCREW-UP*, and I wanted hand gestures, back and forth, *I connect what you're saying to something true inside myself.*

Mom knocked on my door. "You okay, sweetie?"

"Yeah," I croaked.

She opened it. "What are you doing out of bed?"

I was at my desk, in front of my computer. I'd been staring at my screen for the last hour because it didn't even feel like there was a virtual place in the world where I'd be welcome.

"You need to get some rest. There aren't many ailments that can't be cured or at least made better by a good night's sleep."

I nodded.

"To bed soon, mister."

"Okay. Hey, Mom?"

"Yes, honey?"

"Remember when Natalie was a baby and we used to go to the movies on Saturday nights?"

"Of course I remember."

"How come we don't do that anymore?"

She reached over and put a hand to my forehead, convinced I must be running a fever. "Because you got older and had other things you wanted to do."

"Let's go to a movie together. Next weekend. Okay?"

"Okay. I'll even let you choose."

She kissed the top of my head and closed my door behind her. I looked at my phone. Still no text from Daphne. I'd texted her only once, from the platform at Mariachi Plaza.

Me: I'm sorry. I can explain. I want to tell you everything.

Her:

I couldn't say all I needed to in a text: that though I'd lied about nearly everything from the first moment we'd met, I hadn't lied about not knowing she was Juana's daughter, and I hadn't lied when I told her that I loved her.

My screen saver was a picture I'd taken of Daphne's wrist tattoo, and I wished harder than I'd ever wished for anything that Daphne and I had met online because of our shared interest in tattoo photography. What a simple, uncomplicated story.

And I wished that I'd taken the time, just a few minutes, maybe one evening at Penny's kitchen counter while Juana was busy frying her famous potatoes, to say: "Tell me something about your life. Who are you when you aren't in the Brockaways' kitchen?" Over the past two years, we'd talked about food and cooking. We'd talked about Spanish if I was doing homework there. I knew she hated the movies Penny loved because she'd roll her eyes at me when Penny wasn't looking. I knew she could sew because she once fixed a hem on Penny's dress while she was wearing it, and she was pretty good with electronics too. She liked me, I could tell, and she'd ask questions about my parents and my sister, and I never asked her the same questions about her life.

Penny was right about me. I didn't think about things. I never thought about Juana's life outside that too-big house. Not once. This was something I wasn't sure Daphne could forgive me for, and I knew I'd never forgive myself.

I opened up a blank document. Maybe I'd write Daphne a letter. Try to explain everything: the person I was and the person I was trying to be and everything she'd come to mean to me. I stared at all that whiteness for a few minutes before clicking on the little red x that made the blank page go away.

I logged on to *itainteasybeinoffgreen*. The nameless addict from a nameless state now had a nameless girlfriend. He'd met someone who appreciated the sober him, the real, honest him, and things were starting to come together because, finally, after so many mistakes, he was living his life truthfully. I'd discovered him while looking for someone's story to steal, someone whose problems had led him down a path of darkness to a near dead end, and now . . . we'd reversed roles.

Reading his recent entry only made me feel worse, because here I sat, petty and bitter, resenting his turn of good fortune. Was this what it meant to be interconnected in the digital age?

Sunday brought more of the same. Me in my room feeling sad and sorry for myself. I didn't call or text my friends. I didn't ride the bus west toward the beach. I stayed in bed and stared at my phone.

Her:

Nothing.

Will drove me home from school Monday, Maggie riding shotgun with her hand on his knee.

"Dude. You don't look so good."

"Yeah, River. You look . . ." Maggie tilted her head. "Beaten down."

I blamed my fake illness and then fake-coughed. Will and Maggie shielded their faces. "Go get in bed. You need rest."

I walked in the door, put down my backpack and sensed something amiss. The house should have been empty, but somebody was home. I could feel it. Maybe it was a recently brewed cup of coffee or the buzz of a stereo just shut off.

"Hello?" I called.

Silence.

"Hello?"

I walked through the kitchen and living room, past Natalie's room—her door was open, her bed perfectly made because Natalie was a total neat freak—to my room. Mom was sitting on my bed with her face in her hands.

My drawers and closet were open, rifled through, my desk a mess of papers.

"What the hell?"

"Don't you swear at me, River Anthony Dean. Don't you even open your mouth. Don't you stand there," and Mom started to cry, "and put on that indignant face. I've respected your privacy and cut you a lot of slack in your adolescence because . . . I trusted you. I trusted you."

"Mom? What's going on?"

She was full-on sobbing. "I trusted you, River. But I guess I can only blame myself. I tried to be the best mother I could be, but I must have fallen asleep on the job."

The front door opened. "I'm here," Leonard called. In a

flash he was standing beside me in the doorway, still wearing his tool belt. "I came as fast as I could."

"Is someone going to tell me what's going on here?"

Leonard moved inside and sat next to Mom on my bed. He fumbled in his pocket for a wadded-up tissue and handed it to her. He looked at me with his kind, wrinkly eyes.

"Sandra Brockaway called your mom a little while ago."

"I was at work," Mom added, wiping her nose with Leonard's nasty tissue. "Just sitting at my desk."

"She called because she's concerned about you, River."

"Mrs. Brockaway? Concerned about me? That's funny, because I'm pretty sure she hates my guts."

"Well, she's concerned because it's come to her attention that . . . you have a drug problem."

I couldn't help myself—I started laughing, which made Mom cry harder.

"This is not funny, River. Not funny at all."

"Oh yes it is."

Mom looked at Leonard: *DO SOMETHING.*

"Listen, buddy," he said in his man-to-man-voice. "We love you, okay? That's what's most important. And we want to help you."

"I don't need help."

"I know you've been going to meetings, and that's a start—" Mom said.

"I can explain." I was getting tired of hearing myself say this.

"I guess I could have predicted trouble, even though you always seemed so well adjusted, and so responsible, but I know what you've been through with your shit-stain of a father—"

"Mom!" Mom never swore, and certainly never used such gross-out language.

"I'm sorry, but I'm angry, River. Not at you, but at the life you were handed."

"Mom . . . wait. Please." I started laughing again and she glared at me. Leonard took her hand.

I rolled my desk chair across the room and sat facing them. "I'm not addicted to marijuana."

"But Sandra said—"

"I know what Sandra Brockaway said. She said I've been attending meetings at a support group for kids struggling with addiction."

"And you haven't been?"

"Well, I have been, but not because I'm addicted to marijuana."

"So what are you addicted to?" Mom looked panicked. Horrified.

"Nothing. I swear. I'm not addicted to anything."

"So why do you go?"

It was so difficult to know how to answer this question that I opted for the simplest explanation. "Because I like the meetings."

"River." Mom took a deep breath, grabbed a pillow from my bed and squeezed it in her lap. "You're lying."

"No, I'm not!"

"Yes, you are."

"Hold on, everyone," Leonard said. "Let's just stay calm."

Mom looked around my ransacked room. "I went through your things. Maybe that seems like a violation to you, but someday when you're a parent and someone calls you at work to tell you that your son is a drug addict, God help you if you don't rip his room to shreds searching for evidence."

"So . . . what?" I held my arms up in the air. "You didn't find anything."

"That's not exactly true."

I did a quick inventory in my head of what I had hidden in my drawers. Condoms, but Leonard had given those to me, so I could hardly get in trouble for having them, especially since not a single one of them was missing from the box. I couldn't think of anything else incriminating.

"I went on your computer."

"So?"

"So I learned that the time you aren't spending Googling your father you spend on a website devoted to marijuana addiction."

"Oh."

"Gotcha."

"No, I . . . I read that blog so that I could be better at pretending to have an addiction to marijuana. I read it as inspiration. He's like my muse or something." They looked at me, bewildered. "I know this all sounds crazy."

"It sounds unbelievable, is what it sounds."

"Yeah." I rotated in my desk chair. "I guess it does."

"So you've never smoked marijuana?"

There were only two answers to this question. Yes and no. The difficult answer and the easy way out. The truth and the lie. It would have been much simpler for everyone involved if I'd lied, but I knew if I wanted to start fixing everything I had to embrace the truth.

"Only twice."

A long silence followed.

"You can hardly call that addiction," Leonard mumbled.

"Honestly, I didn't like it all that much. Well, I sorta liked it the first time, but the second time was pretty awful. This was a while ago."

Another long silence.

"Even if I'm to believe you about the drugs, River, there's so much more you've lied to us about."

"Like . . ."

"Like where you've been going on Saturday nights. And this girl you've been dating, who's been arrested for shoplifting and happens to be the daughter of Penny's housekeeper."

"I didn't know she was Juana's daughter."

"Sandra Brockaway said she'd prefer if you stayed away from Penny."

"Done."

"And she'd like you to stay away from that girl too."

"Her name is Daphne, and that's something I don't think I can do."

"Sandra Brockaway feels it's inappropriate."

"I'm sorry she feels that way, but it's really none of her goddamn business."

Mom sighed. "I don't know what to think anymore, River."

"Why don't we just take a break?" Leonard was always so even-keeled. Sometimes I wondered what life would have been like without him, if it had just been Mom and me. He, and of course Natalie, had given us a second chance at family. "Let's retreat to our corners for a while, okay? Later tonight after your sister is asleep and we've all had some time to clear our heads, we'll talk again. And River?"

"Yes?"

"You will tell us everything. No more lying. No more obfuscating. No more manipulation of the truth."

NiNETEEN

I started with the sign. I asked them if they'd ever had a moment where it felt like the universe had stepped in front of them, blocked their paths, wrested the wheel from their hands and said: *Here. This. Now.*

They looked at each other and nodded. I like to think they imagined the moment when Leonard, decked out in a mock turtleneck, got a call to bid on an office remodel and said *yes* even though it was a smaller job than he typically took because something about it just felt right.

I walked them through everything that had happened after I stepped into that first meeting, ending with Daphne and Juana at the baseball diamond. I told them that though I could maybe understand Mrs. Brockaway believing I was involved in some elaborate plot to worm my way back into Penny's life, she couldn't be further from the truth.

"What a mess you've gotten yourself into," Leonard said, as if I didn't know this already.

"You're grounded," Mom added.

I just sat there and nodded because I didn't have the will to fight for myself and because I knew Mom felt she had to do something, and this was far better than making me go talk to Sandra Brockaway or any number of other humiliating acts she could have forced me to do.

"And I'm taking away your phone."

I saw a flash of disapproval cross Leonard's face, but he wasn't the disciplinarian. Despite the fact that he'd been in my life now for eleven years, some tasks still fell to Mom.

"Fine." I handed it to her with one final fruitless glance at the screen to see if Daphne had texted me.

Mom stood up and left the room and Leonard lingered for a minute.

"You'll sort this out, River." He ran his hand over his face and pulled on his chin a little. I'd exhausted him. "There is always a way through the thicket."

"Leonard . . . I want you to know . . . that stuff about me Googling my father . . . I . . ."

He reached over and took hold of my shoulders, pulled me toward him and hugged me.

"Don't worry, kid. There's always a way through."

Penny was waiting for me at my locker the next morning. I slowed to a shuffle as I approached her.

"Hi, Pen."

"River. Oh my god."

"Yeah, I know."

"I can't believe. I had no idea. When did you start with the drugs? Was it while we were together?"

I sighed. "I don't really have a drug problem."

"And Daphne? Oh my god."

"I know."

"So when I rejected you, you decided to go after Juana's daughter? What if I'd had a sister? Would you have tried dating her?"

That Penny dared to compare Daphne to a sister demonstrated a whole new level of nerve. She'd seen me with Daphne at the dance and had no idea she was Juana's daughter because in the two years Juana had been working for the Brockaways nobody had ever asked to see a picture of her family.

"Did you even know Juana had kids?"

"Yeah. I knew she had some. We gave her extra bonus money at Christmastime and stuff. You know, for gifts."

"How nice of you."

"How creepy that you tried dating her daughter."

"How convenient to flatter yourself when it had nothing at all to do with you."

Her eyes turned icy and cold, a look I'd only seen a handful of times, when she thought I was paying too much attention to someone else, or if I said something rude. I'd never intentionally been rude to Penny, until this very minute.

"So if it had nothing to do with me, then what's this about?"

"It's about *me*, Penny. It's about what *I* want."

"You just happened to want Juana's daughter?"

"Her name is Daphne. And I don't want *her*, because she's not . . . I don't know . . . an accessory. I just . . . want to be with her as much as I can and I want to know her in the way I never knew you."

"You knew me."

"I just wanted to please you. And do whatever I could to keep you. I was terrified you'd abandon me. Because, like you said, I have issues."

"So you really didn't go after Juana's daughter to somehow get closer to me?"

"Penny . . . I loved you, okay? And you broke my heart. And I'd have done anything to get you back. Anything. That's why I kept showing up at your house with chicken soup or my sister, or anything to get you to remember what a nice boyfriend I'd been to you. I was desperate, yes, but not so desperate that I'd have tracked down Juana's daughter. For one thing: what kind of strategy is that? It's just plain stupid. Believe it or not, it was a total coincidence that I met Daphne. It was at a support group for a drug addiction I don't have—a whole long story I'll tell you some other time—but the important thing to know is that I love her. I *loved* you, but I *love* her. And I get it now, why you broke up with me, I get it, because you were right, I wasn't the person you deserved. I didn't think about things and I just did whatever you wanted me to do and in the end, who wants that? That's not what real relationships are about. The problem now is that I'm not so sure I'm the person Daphne deserves either, and that just makes me unbelievably sad."

The bell rang right then but we just stood at my locker, staring at each other. More than the moment in the middle of the lake, or when I wouldn't let go of the rope, or when she didn't drink the soup I'd brought her, or when I saw her dancing with Evan Lockwood, this felt like the moment when my relationship with Penny Brockaway really, truly ended for good.

I had to go straight home from school as part of my punishment. Maggie drove me that first day, and maybe because she'd seen me through my major life transitions, she was the friend I wanted to come clean to first. All our lives together she'd felt a little like an older, wiser sister.

I took my time. We puttered along many miles under the speed limit—she couldn't listen intently and accelerate simultaneously. I hadn't even gotten to the part about Daphne being Juana's daughter when we pulled in front of my house. I was still explaining the meetings, and why I'd lied about the Instagram account, Daphne's arrest for shoplifting and my fake weed addiction.

"But I had to throw water in your face the last time you smoked pot. You're the world's most irritating stoned person."

"Yeah, I know."

She shifted into park and shut off the engine. "I guess I

just don't understand how anyone could buy *you* as a drug addict."

I sighed. "They didn't know me. I could be anybody I wanted to be."

"You could be anyone you wanted to be and that's who you chose?"

She opened the door to get out of the car.

"I'm grounded. You can't come in."

"What? Why are you grounded?"

"I'm getting to that part."

It was important to me not to violate Mom's rules (straight home from school, no friends over, no phone calls or texts), so I'd found a loophole by sitting with Maggie in her car in front of my house, which we did for the next forty-five minutes. I told her everything, ending with me and Penny at my locker.

"Holy crap storm."

"And I've got no umbrella."

She sighed. "Oh, River . . ."

I knew there was a follow-up to this *Oh, River,* because Maggie always told it like it was. Once, when we were five, she asked if I wanted to borrow her dad. I said I already had one. *You don't have a dad,* she told me, just like that, full of blunt truth, and I never, ever thought about my father the same way again.

". . . you can be such an egregious asshole."

"Okay . . . not quite what I expected."

"What *did* you expect? Why on earth did you think any

of this was okay? In what universe did you think it was fair to go to meetings for kids with real problems and fake an addiction? And lie to everyone? Your family? Your friends?"

"I was confused. I was just trying to sort out my life. Make some sense of everything."

"Great job with that."

I put my head on her shoulder. I knew it would soften her, and also, I needed the closeness.

"How are you going to fix this, River?"

"I don't know. It doesn't really seem like flowers will do the trick."

"Flowers never do the trick. They're totally lame. And who are these flowers for, anyway? Daphne? Is she the only one who matters here? What about everybody else?"

"You're right. But what do I do? I don't know what to do."

She put her hand on my head and gave me the sort of squeeze that let me know that in the end, things would be okay. Between us. And I hoped everywhere else too.

"What you need to do, River, is grow up."

TWENTY

The easiest place to start was the most obvious. If I wanted to grow up, I was going to have to get my driver's license. I couldn't continue to rely on other people. It was time to start navigating the city and my life on my own.

Because my eighteenth birthday was coming up soon, I could get a permit without taking driver's ed, which only proved that laziness and procrastination sometimes reap rewards. Leonard was so thrilled he immediately took me to get a permit, cleared his afternoons for the rest of the week, picked me up at school each day in his truck and took me out for practice. It wasn't anything like you see in the movies where a father and son kick up dust as they drive down a dirt road or meander in circles around a big empty parking lot. This was Los Angeles. There were no dirt roads, no empty parking lots.

We started in our neighborhood and ventured out a little farther each afternoon, finally ending our week in Westwood Village, where I parallel parked and we went to the deli for mediocre pastrami sandwiches. We chose a table by the window.

"I'll tell you something if you promise not to tell your mother," he said to me.

"Okay."

"I've been checking your texts."

"And?"

He shook his head.

I shrugged. "She was never a big texter. It's one of the things I really liked about her. She preferred talking."

"Well, she hasn't called you either."

"Leonard, are you trying to kick me when I'm down?"

"No." He popped open his can of cream soda and held it out. I clinked mine against his, as was our tradition. "I just wanted you to know that she's not trying to reach you and wondering if you're ignoring her."

I pushed my pastrami sandwich away from me. "I've ruined everything."

"Give it time."

"I thought it was fate."

"Fate?"

"Yeah. I thought it was fate that led me to her. I'd never believed in fate. Stars never aligned for me. But then I wandered in there that night. And there was Daphne. Fate, right?"

He nodded noncommittally.

"And now I've screwed it all up. I've ruined fate. I've pissed on it. Or worse—I've reversed it. She's never going to talk to me again."

Leonard took his time chewing. "You know what I think, Riv?"

"Nope."

"I think fate has nothing at all to do with any of this. I think fate is bullshit. You want to know the real force behind what happens to you in your life?"

"I guess."

"Heredity. Who your parents are. Even who your grandparents were. And you've already bucked that force, because you're nothing like your father. You're someone who believes deeply in connection, in real human, person-to-person connection. That's what happened to you with Daphne. You connected with someone, and it might feel like that's because of some otherworldly force, like fate or whatever you want to name it, but you took risks, albeit some really stupid risks, and you opened yourself up to her and, well . . . that's what makes this life worth living. Connections like that. So you can't now go blame fate and shrug and say *I guess it wasn't meant to be.* Obstacles arose, as obstacles will. You have to go and hurdle them, because if you leave it all to fate you're ceding control to a force that's made up. You have to believe in the power of your connections."

We sat in silence for a few minutes while Leonard ate his sandwich and I let what he'd said sink in.

"Thanks, Leonard. You know, for the driving lessons and everything."

"If you don't stop thanking me I'll never let your mother give you your phone back."

Mom and Leonard still referred to the "day college letters come," everyone did, because language can't keep pace with technology, but the truth is that before letters would come I could log on to websites to which I'd been given passwords to uncover whether I'd been invited to be a member of the incoming freshman class.

That day was a Friday.

I knew I should have been counting forward to this day, but instead I counted backward: it had been 13 whole days, 312 whole hours since I'd spoken to Daphne Vargas. She was the person I wanted to call to tell that I'd gotten into four of the five schools I'd heard from.

Mom and Leonard were waiting for me out in the kitchen. Celebratory waffles were cooked. Powdered sugar on top. Natalie double-checked the spelling of the word *university* for a card she was planning on making later. It felt good, exciting even, but mostly I just saw my different futures at four distinct points on a map, four plane rides away from the city I was just learning to navigate on my own.

I hadn't heard yet from the University of California schools. Mom had gone to UC Santa Barbara and Leonard to Berkeley. I'd applied to both, as well as UCLA and San Diego, in addition to the five private schools I'd already heard from. It wasn't like Mom and Leonard had discouraged me from going to UC, it was more that they figured since tuition wasn't a concern, what with Thaddeus Dean footing the bill, why not an East Coast or Chicago school?

We had the day off. They called it teacher training day, but really the administration knew emotions in the senior class would be running high and they wanted to avoid the drama. Some would have gotten just what they wanted. Others would be crushed. Many would be recalculating. This wasn't a magic wish-granting bus where anything could happen. Some doors had opened and others had slammed shut.

What was next for me? What did I want?

I wanted more time. I wanted time to slow down. I wanted time to slow down so much that it moved backward so I could undo the mess I'd made.

Mom returned my phone. I was allowed to go out with my friends to celebrate our college news.

I called around but couldn't reach anyone. I sent texts. It was Friday night. A big Friday night. Will, Luke and Maggie had to be together figuring out their plans.

I dropped by Luke's house. His mom answered the door. She was dressed for work in a suit, but with a University of Michigan beanie on her head.

"Hi, Dr. Torres."

"River!" She gave me a long hug. "How'd it go?"

"Pretty good. Still weighing options."

She pointed at her hat. "So proud of Lukey. Go Blue!"

"That's great news."

"They left here about a half hour ago. You must be running late? They took some pizzas with them. I think they were headed to the beach. Can you believe this weather? You must know where they're going. Which beach?"

"Yes, I know."

"Do you need me to run you over to meet them?" Even Luke's mom had to give me rides sometimes.

"No thanks, it's okay. I can get there myself."

I hopped a bus to Santa Monica. The sun was just going down when I found them at the same lifeguard tower where Maggie had thrown the water in my face so I'd stop asking, through my stoned haze, how much time was going by. They sat barefoot, legs dangling off the side of the tower, watching the sunset.

I stood below them, looking up. They'd finished off the pizza and half a six-pack of beer.

"You made it," Will called down.

"It wasn't easy." I picked up two fistfuls of sand and let it fall through my fingers.

"You lied to us," Luke said. "About pretty much everything."

"I know." I sat in the sand. "I'm . . . beyond sorry."

Will threw a can of beer down to me, but I didn't open it.

"I would have told you guys, but I didn't know how."

Luke leaned over the railing. "How hard would it have been to say *I'm faking a drug addiction to get close to a girl?*"

"It was more complicated than that. But that's not an excuse. I should have told you."

"Yeah, River," Will said. "You should have."

"I know."

"Because," he added, "we're friends."

"Still?"

"At least until we scatter around the country to different

schools and make newer, better, more lasting friendships." Luke and Maggie slugged him.

I climbed the tower and sat next to Maggie.

"Dude," Luke said. "Are you okay coming here? You aren't worried about flashbacks?"

"Are you thinking about using again?" Will leaned in. "Do I need to call your sponsor?"

The last of the light was leaving the sky. The ocean dark and vast before us. I lay on my back on the lifeguard tower with my legs dangling off the edge and looked up at the stars. There weren't many to see.

"So, you guys," I said. "I don't want any of you to freak out or anything, but since I'm being honest now, there's something I have to tell you."

"Okay," they said. They waited.

"I'm getting my driver's license."

"Whoa," Will said. "That's harder to imagine than you as a drug addict."

Maggie took a swig of beer. "This is not the world I know and inhabit. I'm feeling . . . unsafe." I stood up and started unbuttoning my jeans. "Uh . . . what are you doing? Now I'm feeling *extremely* unsafe," she said.

I dropped my pants and kicked them off and stood in Will's short-shorts. Will and Luke and Maggie stared for a minute before lifting their beers in a toast.

"Take a lap of shame, River Dean," Will said.

I climbed down from the tower and ran toward the horizon, my friends cheering me on.

TWENTY-ONE

The next night, Saturday, I walked to a dreary stretch of midcity Pico, to a building with a faded, tattered white awning onto which the words A SECOND CHANCE were painted in black.

I waited across the street until the meeting let out, dying for a glimpse of Daphne, even the shortest one would do, though she wasn't the person I'd come here to see.

Christopher stepped outside and lit a cigarette. Mason kept him company. Everyone else dispersed to idling cars or around corners and I started to wonder if Daphne had skipped out on the meeting, but then, finally, the doors opened and there she stood.

Somehow I expected her to look different, because it felt like a lifetime since I'd seen her. I wanted to call her name, but I hid in the building's shadow and watched as the three of them climbed into Christopher's car and sped off to the east.

A few more minutes passed, and then the lights turned

off and Everett stepped out with his ring of keys and started to lock the glass doors.

I jaywalked across Pico. Someone slammed on his horn just as I reached the safety of the curb. Everett spun around.

"Hi," I said.

"Hi, River."

A long silence followed.

"Are you here to tell me why you've missed the last few meetings?"

"Daphne didn't say anything?"

"About you? No." He secured the ring of keys to his belt loop, folded his arms across his chest and eyed me from beneath his bushy brows. "This looks serious."

"It is. Can we, like, go somewhere? Can I buy you a cup of coffee or something?"

He gazed at me in that way he did that always made me want to look away. "I don't drink coffee."

"Oh, okay."

"I drink tea."

We walked to a restaurant two blocks away: an old steakhouse with red leather booths and filthy green carpeting that both time and customers seemed to have forgotten. Most of the tables were empty, and the man who greeted us in his white dinner jacket seemed neither bothered nor thrilled to serve us tea and nothing else.

"I really appreciate you hearing me out. I know your time is valuable and that you already give it generously."

"Thank you for recognizing that."

"So I'll just cut to the chase."

"Please do."

"I'm not addicted to marijuana."

He sipped his tea and said nothing.

"I lied. About that and about pretty much everything else. And I kissed Daphne and kinda fell in love with her."

He didn't react, so I continued to talk. Faster and faster.

"I wish I'd known how to tell the truth that first night, but I was too embarrassed. I wandered in because I saw the sign and I felt lost and alone and dumped. How lame is that? Everyone else had real problems and mine seemed so small and stupid. And then, somehow, being there just . . . helped, but more than helped, it became important and . . . meaningful, I guess. So maybe it wasn't just getting dumped that brought me to the group, maybe I really did, or do, need help with other things. I know this probably doesn't make much sense. But anyway, I wanted to apologize. I messed up. Daphne hates me now and I'm guessing everyone else will too. I violated the rules. All of them."

"Why are you telling me this?"

I didn't understand the question, so I pulled an Everett and stared back at him without saying anything.

"Why didn't you just stop coming to meetings? Why didn't you disappear? You wouldn't have been the first person to stop showing up. Why bother admitting everything to me? Why bother buying me tea?"

"Because I feel bad. Terrible, actually. And I wanted

to try in my own stupid way to make things right, even though I know I can't. But still I wanted to try. Because I don't want to let perfect be the enemy of good. I'm trying to do good by telling the truth."

"So . . . honesty. That's why you're here. To deliver a dose of honesty."

"I guess so."

"That's a start."

He sipped his tea again. "So Mason was right about you all along. You're full of shit."

"Yes."

Everett laughed a little. "Don't be so quick to agree. Defend yourself."

"I can't, really."

"I believe that you came to the group in the midst of a struggle, I could see that about you. You were in some pain. That was real. I don't know what it is and I don't know if you do either, but you should figure that out. Just . . . not with us."

"Okay. But I still want to make it right. To tell the truth and say I'm sorry. Maybe people will forgive me. Mason won't, I know, but maybe the others will?"

He refilled his cup from the pot between us. "River, when you apologize you acknowledge that you've caused someone hurt. That's it. You can't do it with the expectation that you'll be forgiven. You have to apologize simply because you want to."

He was right. Obviously. That was why he was the group's leader and I was the group's impostor.

"So it's okay if I come to the meeting next week? I don't want to intrude. I've done enough of that already."

He cleared his throat. "River . . ." He stopped. "Wait a minute . . . is River even your real name?"

"Improbably, yes it is."

"River, you are cordially invited to attend next Saturday night's meeting of A Second Chance group for teens. Your presence is kindly requested at six-forty sharp."

"But the meetings start at six-thirty."

"I'm going to do you a solid and put them all on notice."

What I didn't tell Everett was that by the next group meeting, the following Saturday, I'd be eighteen years old. My actual birthday was on Thursday, but Mom and Leonard had planned a dinner at the house Saturday with my friends to celebrate. I asked if we could switch the party to Friday instead. Natalie looked disappointed.

"But we already planned it for Saturday. I picked out the paper plates."

"So? Friday is even sooner. The paper plates you picked will be just as awesome on Friday."

"I'd have to switch around a work thing . . . ," Mom said. "But what's wrong, suddenly, with Saturday?" I could tell she was aiming for curious rather than suspicious.

"Well, it's just that I want to go back to A Second Chance."

Mom shot Leonard a look. Something along the lines of: *See? I told you the kid was a pothead.*

"Christ, Mom! I swear. Read my lips: I am not addicted to drugs. I don't know what else to say. Do you want me to pee in a cup?"

"Why would you pee in a cup? Gross. And why would Mom think you like drugs?"

I'd momentarily forgotten that Natalie was in the room, and that she was only eight.

"I'm just joking around, Nat. I'd never pee in a cup. At least not in any of the cups you use." I made a goofy face at her. "And Mom teases me about drugs just because I like to go to these meetings to help kids with their problems."

"That's weird."

"Mom's weird."

"Hey!" Mom protested.

"But River," Natalie said. "You have other problems you could talk about in your meetings."

I reached over and put my hand on Natalie's head. It still fit perfectly into my palm, though it wouldn't forever.

"You're right, Nat. I do have problems."

"It's okay. Everyone has problems."

"Not you. You're perfect."

I heard from the UC schools on my birthday. I was accepted to all except Berkeley, where I hoped they'd given the spot to Maggie that they didn't offer me, though I understood it didn't really work that way.

I called her immediately.

"Can't talk," she chirped. "On with Will. I'm in. I'm in! Happy birthday, Riv."

"Thanks, Mags."

I stared at the home screen on my phone. I scrolled through my contacts and lingered on Daphne's name. I'd composed a thousand texts and deleted them, each one some version of *I'm sorry* or *Let me explain* or *Give me a chance.*

It was my birthday, and with a heart full of useless hope I wondered if she'd call, or text. Something simple.

It was a birthday wish that didn't come true.

TWENTY-TWO

On the afternoon of my eighteenth birthday, after I aced the written and road tests, the California Department of Motor Vehicles issued a temporary driver's license to River Anthony Dean. On the same day, I filed papers to change my last name to Marks to match my family. To harness the force of that heredity.

When my new, permanent license came, with my new, permanent name, I planned on slipping it underneath Natalie's door in a construction paper card decorated with glitter.

On Friday I had all my best friends over. Mom made my favorite lasagna and Maggie baked a cake she decorated to look like a driver's license. We ate off Natalie's paper plates, which had Spider-Man on them because once upon a time I'd loved Spider-Man, and Natalie was still at the age where she believed when you love something you love it forever.

On Saturday night I drove myself to the meeting at A Second Chance—my first solo trip in Leonard's truck.

At six-thirty-five I sat parked on Pico across from the sign I'd spotted on that long, lonely walk home on a night which felt like a lifetime ago. That sign that I'd seen lit up like Vegas or Times Square. That SIGN—big, bright, flashing like neon—glowed again for me tonight as I stared at it from behind the wheel of Leonard's truck.

A SECOND CHANCE.

It turned out to be a SIGN after all, but it hadn't promised a second chance with Penny, it promised a second chance with me.

I stepped out of the truck, grabbed my shopping bags and walked up to the glass doors, where I stopped to read the message again.

HERE: Is where you belong.

THIS: Is where change begins.

NOW: Is the time.

I opened the doors and went inside.

No audible gasps. No dropped jaws. No whispering *He's here?* But also: no smiles. No calls of "Hey, River." No hand motions back and forth.

An empty seat in the circle awaited me. Daphne sat four chairs to the left. I didn't try making eye contact; I couldn't bear to watch her look away.

I walked to the center of the circle and unpacked the bags, passing the contents around. I handed Christopher the lukewarm French dip from Philippe's I'd picked up earlier in the day. Bree got the rainbow carrots and a honey-thyme goat cheese spread from Whole Foods. I gave Mason kettle corn from the Santa Monica Pier because he'd talked one time about his foster mom taking him there on the day they met. I brought an assortment of high-end herbal teas for Everett, and for Daphne: a strawberry Jarritos and a bag of fresh tortilla chips from the taqueria on Venice where we'd dined under the fairy lights the night I first rode the bus. I passed around the other stuff.

I'd been nervous all week, but now that I had lowered myself into the metal folding chair and had taken a deep breath and was beginning to tell my story, my real story, I felt the same sort of peace I'd come to know over the past few months of Saturday nights.

I talked more than I had in all the previous meetings combined. Nobody rolled their eyes or looked away, not even Mason. And some of them, I noticed, quietly ate the snacks I'd brought. "Even if I'd had the courage to tell the truth that night when I first came here"—I was finishing up—"I didn't understand. I thought it was Penny. I thought it was getting dumped. But being here each week taught me it was more. You all made me . . . a better person." I stopped, took a few breaths. Battled the frog inside. "And it's important to me that you know that even though I failed in here as a sharer, I listened. I heard you all. Every one of you. And . . . I'm sorry for all the lies."

I croaked that last *I'm sorry*. A few tears escaped and I wiped them away.

I stood up, folded my chair, and stacked it against the wall.

"Hey, River."

I turned around. Mason.

"I hope you never show your ugly, lying face in here again. But before you go . . ." He sighed and looked at the popcorn in his lap. "A-plus for snacks."

I walked out of the building, climbed into Leonard's truck. I didn't need the rain or Will's sappy music—I drove home, crying all the way.

I woke early the next morning. Mom and Leonard were still asleep. So was Natalie. I did something next that I knew wasn't going to win me their faith, trust or goodwill: I took Leonard's truck without asking, leaving a note that said I'd be back later, I'd be careful, and that I was sorry but I didn't want to wake anyone.

I drove to the same café in Venice where I'd cobbled together a text of tattoos for Daphne—*CALL ME*—and I ordered coffee and toast. Thaddeus Dean's presentation at the Barton Center Conference on Interconnectedness and Conflict Resolution didn't start until eleven o'clock. I had some time to spare.

I suppose I knew the minute I saw him on the conference schedule—smirking from behind his square-framed glasses, arms folded across his chest, leaning back casually against a brick wall—that I'd go see him. Maybe approach him after his lecture, while the headset still kept that stupid little microphone in place. Maybe he'd look at me like I was just another young wannabe tech entrepreneur hoping to catch a little of his magic. *Yes?* He'd say. *What would you like to know?*

Or maybe he'd see me and recognize his own features staring back at him and he'd stick out his hand or even open his arms to me. *River!* He'd say. *My boy! My son! Look how big you've grown!*

I didn't know what to expect when I finally saw him face to face. None of the scenarios I played out in my head included me standing alone outside the Barton Center because the conference had been sold out for months.

The guard whose job it was to keep out the likes of me had no sympathy. He blocked my path with his clipboard and expressionless face.

"I just . . . I need to talk to Thaddeus Dean. Please. It's really, really important."

The crowd behind me was large and growing, people with their legitimizing badges on strings around their necks.

"Sorry, kid."

"You don't seem sorry."

He glared at me.

"I'm just saying that didn't feel like a real apology. When you apologize you acknowledge that you've caused someone hurt . . . and it doesn't seem like you're acknowledging that you're hurting me."

"Step aside."

I did, but only about a half step. I thought of entering through another doorway, trying my luck with a different gatekeeper, but instead I stood like a rock in the middle of a raging tide. When everyone else had been allowed into the building, the man turned to face me again.

He looked me up and down. "Is this guy really *all that*?"

It was an excellent question. It was, in fact, *THE QUESTION*. Was Thaddeus Dean really all that?

"He's my father."

"Then why don't you have a badge?"

"He hasn't seen me in, like, twelve years."

He stared at me. "You got some ID?"

I took out my new license. "See? My last name is Dean too. For now at least. I'm changing it."

He turned it over, handed it back, shrugged and opened the door for me. "Be my guest."

The auditorium was packed, some people sitting on the floor, legs folded like eager preschoolers. I stood in the very back. The lights finally dimmed and a spotlight shone down onto an empty stage; thunderous applause filled the room as Thaddeus Dean stepped into it.

"Thank you. Thanks. Really thank you." Hands to chest. A little bowing of the head. "Thank you. Thank you very much."

"When I was a small child," he began, "I dreamed big."

He continued, and I thought: *When I was a small child . . . I wondered where my father had gone.*

When I was a small child . . . I was forced to see a therapist with smudged glasses whose office reeked of patchouli.

When I was a small child . . . I refused Maggie's offer to borrow her father because I believed I still had my own.

If heredity is the best indicator of what happens to you

in life, then things were looking up for me. I'd given heredity the slip. I was soon to become River Anthony Marks. Someone who believes, deep down, in the power of real human, person-to-person connection.

I was nothing like my father. He had nothing to teach me. I had nothing to learn from him. And so in the middle of Thaddeus Dean's speech, I left. The way through the thicket on this morning was beneath the exit sign. I walked out of the auditorium, pushing open the heavy doors and letting them close behind me. I'd hoped for a *slam*, but all I got was a *whoosh*.

TWENTY-THREE

My eyes took a moment to adjust to the midday sun and then another moment to make sense of what I saw.

Daphne.

Sitting alone on a concrete bench.

She stood up slowly and waved, her silver-painted nails catching the light.

I rushed over and asked the world's most obvious question. "What are you doing here?"

"I had a feeling," she said. "I just . . . I know you, River, and I knew you wouldn't be able to stay away. And I thought you might need someone. You know, afterward."

"But how did you—"

"You aren't the only one with Google."

I sighed and sat down on the bench, suddenly weak all over. She sat next to me but didn't take my hand. If this had been a year ago, or really just a few weeks ago, I would have believed that Daphne had come here today to tell me she loved me too and that nothing mattered but our love and that everything would be okay between us. I would have believed that next we'd get into my truck, we'd buckle our seat belts, and I'd drive her off into the sunset. We'd costar in a perfect ending.

But I'd grown up since then.

"How'd it go in there?"

I thought before I answered. "It was good."

I looked up at her. Her dark, beautiful eyes. "Daphne, I wasn't trying to get back together with Penny. I—"

"I know you weren't, and it doesn't matter anyway. We . . . it was a mess. And I knew I was getting into a mess when we started. You knew it too. We should have listened to those voices. Our better selves. The ones that told us we shouldn't start anything. I hate to admit it, but Everett's pamphlet was right."

I stared at the tattoo of roses on the vine that wound around her beautiful wrist.

"My mom says you're a really nice boy. She says you're a good person even though you made some mistakes."

"And . . . who wants to date a boy her mom thinks is nice?"

She shook her head. "I don't want to date an addict. Whether it's—drugs, love, lying. I can't be with someone who needs me to make him okay with himself. I've had enough of taking care of other people. And really, we need to fix ourselves first. So what I want, River, is to be your friend. I want you to be my friend. And eventually . . . we'll be better people. I hope."

"Daphne, I—"

"I know. You're sorry. I heard you last night. And I believe you. And I know you miss me because, well . . . I miss you too. But that doesn't mean it's all okay, and it doesn't mean we should be together. What it means is you should find another group to go to, or at least someone else to talk to. Something."

After a minute, I nodded.

She finally reached out and took my hand, but she held it in a handshake. "Friends?"

I wanted to hold on to her hand like I'd held on to the rope that day in Echo Park Lake. But I let go.

"I'll try."

"You'll try?"

"Yes. That's the best I can offer: the truth. I'll try to be your friend. A good friend. But I won't give up on the idea that someday . . . you'll see me differently. And when you do, it'll be because—"

"Because you bulked up? Filled out those skinny-ass arms?"

"No!" I nudged her with my shoulder and leaned into her. "It'll be because I earned it."

She smiled.

"And I'm not going far. I'm going to UCLA. Not because I want to save Thaddeus Dean some money, because you're right, he owes me. And not because I'm afraid to go away. And not because of you. I'm going to UCLA because this is where I want to be. Like Everett says. Here. I want to be here. I want this. Now."

"Good for you."

"You're way smarter than me, Daphne. I know you need to take a year off and figure things out. But go to college soon. Get a degree or two or three and then take on the world. I can't wait to watch you do that."

She put up her hand, shielding her eyes from the sun. "Let's go to a diner or something. We'll start with French fries and then take on the world, okay, *guapo*?"

I reached into my pocket and pulled out the keys to Leonard's truck, dangling them in front of her. "I'll drive."

"Look at you!" She snatched the keys, looked them over and tossed them back to me. "My community service project! Getting around this big city all on his own."

I stood up and helped her to her feet. "Without you I'd probably still be waiting at the wrong bus stop."

"Without me you'd probably still be bumming rides."

I laughed. We started across the street.

"Nah . . . River, you didn't need me. You'd have figured it out somehow."

She was right. So was Leonard. There is always a way through the thicket. It might have taken me a little longer if I hadn't met Daphne Vargas, but luckily I had. Was it luck that brought us together? Fate? The stars aligning? Some otherworldly force? Or was it just real human connection?

In the end, it didn't matter. I was going to take this girl out for a plate of French fries.

I held the truck door for her. She climbed in and buckled

her seat belt. I got in behind the wheel. Pulled down the visor because the sun shone right in my eyes, and then I started driving toward it, just like they do in perfect endings.

But this wasn't an ending.

And it wasn't perfect.

It was better than perfect—it was good.